Bro. Abdulla
    Life is too short to enjoy,
have fun.
    Best regards to your mom too,
    & God bless.

            Isauro M. Enverga

The Winged Viper

The Winged Viper

Saurome Series 1 and Series 2

by

Isauro M. Enverga

Eloquent Books

New York, New York

Eloquent Books
An imprint of AEG Publishing Group
845 Third Avenue, 6th Floor - 6016
New York, NY 10022
www.eloquentbooks.com

ISBN: 978-1-60693-967-3   1-60693-967-X

Printed in the United States of America

Book Design: SP

Table of Contents

Part I

Chapter 1—The Meeting..9

Chapter 2—The Origins..17

Chapter 3—Discovering Each Other...19

Chapter 4—Educating the Winged Viper.......................................33

Part II

Chapter 1—The Call..43

Chapter 2—Mafiosi versus Yakuza..49

Chapter 3—The Deal...51

Chapter 4—At the Yakuza HQ...53

Chapter 5—Two Inventions of Dr. Yokohama: Eye of the Eagle
and the Golden Eye..59

Chapter 6—The Proposal...87

Chapter 7—Back at the Safe House..95

Chapter 8—The Meeting...107

Chapter 9—The Ordeal of Dr. Yokohama....................................121

Part III

Chapter 1—France..147

Part I

Chapter 1
The Meeting

In the darkness of the summer night, along the unlighted streets of Santa Monica Beach, a humid, quiet, and moonless, starry sky loomed over the horizon.

A girl, Graconica, was homeless, hungry, and cold. She told herself, *I shall have at least one meal a day,* after she killed the circus manager by hanging him from the high wire.

A few years ago, in her past life, the circus high wire was the place where she had enjoyed walking, dancing, and performing. She was a small and thin girl. It was her turf.

She took the money and the cheeseburger from the table, still warm to the touch, and ran outside.

She needed no planning in carrying out the execution of her target. Using her instinct, she could plan and act on it in a split second.

She went straight to her spot along the beach, where homeless Iraqi and Afghan war veterans slept. It was dark and cold along the shore that night. The sharp wind was whipping her face with her hair. Expressionlessly eating the now-cold cheeseburger, she had a pocketful of money to keep her from being hungry for several days.

She heard the crackling of gunshots in rapid succession from a distance. She lifted her head and stopped chewing to listen to any accompanying sounds. The other sleeping homeless just covered their heads. Then she heard the screeching sound of a car, a door opening and closing, and then silence.

It was long past midnight, and she continued to eat her late meal.

Suddenly, an elderly man in a nice, bloody suit staggered behind her. He was like a drunk ready to stumble. The stranger murmured, "Help me," and fell to the ground.

From a distance, she heard several fast cars as if they were racing, then suddenly brakes sounded on the streets, leaving prominent skid marks on the concrete pavement of the road.

She quickly covered the stranger with sand and made the edges even so that it would just look like an ordinary ground, and continued munching her food, looking from the sides of her eyes. Those guys were not cops, but they wore nice suits, like the fallen guy.

One guy approached her and asked, "Did you see anybody running this way?"

She just gave him a blank stare and the guy left, thinking she was just a half-witted homeless girl. She remembered her mother had said, "Looks can be deceiving."

When she heard the cars speed away, she went to the guy and uncovered his face and asked him, "Are you okay?"

He answered, "Yes. Thank you. Can you help me get to my car, please?"

She stood up and said, "C'mon. Which side shall I hold you?"

"Here on my left," he said.

She saw the bloody right hand; she knew it was wounded somewhere along the line.

"You are strong for your size. My name's Resty. What's yours?"

"Graconica."

"I'll call you Nica; it's easier."

"That's cool."

She walked him to his car.

"If you have no place to stay, come with me to my house. See if you like to stay. I could use a hand while I am mending my own. Do you know how to drive?"

"No."

"How old are you?"

"Fourteen."

She helped Resty sit in the driver's seat and took the passenger's seat.

Resty said, "Now I can use you. Hold that gear, press the button and pull it downward, and put it into D."

She did it with ease. She thought, *That was easy.*

While on the road, Resty started the conversation. "Did you run away from home?"

"No."

"Do you want to tell me?"

"I am not from this country. My parents and I came to the United States as tourists. We went inside something, the Murrah government building, I don't remember exactly, but it was in Oklahoma City. What I can remember is that there was a colorful cotton candy cart passing before we entered that building. I asked my mother if I could buy some, but the cotton candy cart crossed the street, so I ran after it. When I reached the cotton candy guy, I heard a deafening explosion behind me, and I was thrown forward and I remember no more. I don't know how many days, but I woke up in a white tent, like a hospital. I had some bruises and my body ached, but I didn't mind them. Wounded people were all around,

11

crying and moaning all over. I was very confused. I walked around searching for my parents until nightfall, but I did not find them."

"How did you get here?"

"I ride trains, hiding behind the cargo, sometimes dirty pick-ups with farm products. I have nowhere to go."

"Have you been fighting?" Resty asked and pointed with his lips to the bruising on her left check.

"No. I wanted to watch a circus show, but I have no money. When I insisted, the circus manager slapped me so hard that I fell."

In her mind, she wanted to get his sympathy. Because she'd seen the manager's hand coming, she'd been able to block it before it landed on her cheek. She caught it in her left hand and threw herself along with the force, so that it would appear to the onlookers that she was thrown from the force of the slap. The smudge on her face was from her dirty hand; it was not a bruise.

"You did not report it to the police?"

"I don't think any policeman would take my side. All ticket windows carry one and the same principle, 'No money, no entry.'"

"Do you want to get even with that circus manager?"

"No. I've forgiven him."

"You have a big heart, Nica."

She thought, *He is now cold and hanging.*

Dan Spaniel, the circus manager, had a family to feed. It was early that evening when he saw the line moving away from his ticket window. A tiny odorous bum approached. He thought, *She's driving my money away. I'll teach her a lesson.*

He went outside and slapped her so hard and said, "Get away from here, you piece o'shit."

It was a minute past midnight, and Mr. Spaniel was counting the ticket sales. He picked up the phone and ordered a double cheeseburger, large fries with a large diet soda for delivery to his office from a nearby burger place.

He was almost done, and the warm cheeseburger was waiting for him on the table. He remembered the girl he slapped earlier. He thought, *That was strange, she was thrown so far, like in a Superman movie; I am the superman. But whenever I slap my wife, she just falls to the floor, no matter how hard I hit her. Even my children, they don't go that far. When I kicked my youngest yesterday, she was thrown just a few steps from me. Hmm . . . I better try my strength on my little boy tonight to see if I can do that again.*

My wife and my children are useless animals. I feed them, I give them shelter and clothes. I am the only one working. I pay all the insurance. In case I die, they'll swim in money. I better wake them up tonight with a painful kick; then they might think they are having nightmares.

That was the moment when he felt a sting around his neck. It was burning his skin, with excruciating pain, paralyzing his legs. He felt his eyes bulging as if they wanted to go out of their sockets, and he could see his hands shaking. He was being dragged outside his office. Then he saw the floor going away—farther and farther away. He saw the empty benches lined around far below him. He was being lifted and spinning slowly. Then his vision became dark and then white. He could see a blinding brightness; then he remembered no more.

The next day he was found hanging by a thin fishing line.

Resty continued to drive in a less populated area. The line of palm trees and bushes accentuated the darkness of the surroundings until they reached a sharp right turn. No other vehicles were around, and it seemed that it was the usual thing in this area. When they entered the underpass, they went downward in a very fast, forward thrust. They were now under a tunnel. Resty pushed a button, and a gate opened. They entered a long driveway that went under the mansion. Resty pushed another button, and a wall opened. Nica understood that this was a secret door.

Resty understood her hesitation. They entered a hallway. Resty opened the door to their right and said, "Go inside, take a bath and clean up. Help yourself; it's free. I'll wait for you in the dining room in an hour. Try to find your way but don't go out of the house." He said that whatever she found was hers, so that she wouldn't steal anything. He figured she couldn't steal something that she already owned.

She said, "I'll try."

He wanted to ask, *Try what? Finding your way to the dining room or not getting out?* He decided not to ask and went on. He thought, *She looks special, witty, strong, and very quick. She was able to hide me under the sand in a matter of seconds.*

She went inside and closed the door behind her. She scanned the closet; lots of towels, bathrobes, and pajamas, nothing feminine. She went to the bathroom; it was dustless and shiny. She took off her gold necklace with the diamond-studded pendant in the shape of a flower, and then placed it on a safe corner below the mirror. She thought, *He said these are all mine. He calls me Nica. I like that. From now on, that will be my new name: Nica.*

She took a long, warm bath. She scrubbed every inch of her body, especially between her toes and fingers and all her skin folds. She repeated the sequence several times, until she really felt fresh and clean. She felt ten pounds lighter.

After the long and refreshing bath, she dried herself and put on the smallest pajamas she found. She went out of the room and figured out where the dining room was. She followed the smell, and she was right.

A middle-aged man was standing at the end of the table and said, "Miss, my name is Conrado. I am the butler. Mr. Resty will be out in a few minutes."

"You're the boss," she said. "You can also call me Nica." She walked toward the fireplace to warm herself.

She was not that hungry anymore. She extended her arms, feeling the warmth of the fire from her palms and then pressed it against her face repeatedly in graceful, measured intervals.

Resty came, his right arm bandaged and in a sling, and said, "C'mon, girl. Let's have some proper late supper before you go to bed." Resty noticed the tiny red lines that ran around and along Nica's hands up to the arms, a mark of strangulation.

They went to the table. "Conrado, you can leave us now. I'll call you if we need something."

"Why are you not in school?" Resty started.

"I was," she paused and started eating, "where I come from."

"Do you want to go back to school?"

"I study at home."

"I can arrange that."

"Will you do that for me?" Nica said, looking at him.

"Remember, you saved my life."

She smiled. She thought, *I took one and saved one.*

Conrado was in the kitchen, slicing some fruit for dessert. He could not forget the difficult life he had in Colombia, which he called a life of drugs and murders. He hated that kind of life. That was why he ran away. He was able to save fifty dollars, all his life savings. His mother was in tears when he said goodbye. "Where do you want to go, my son?"

"Someplace where I can earn clean money; a decent wage that comes from my sweat and not from the blood and tears of others," he replied.

"And where do you think that place exists? There is no place like that here on earth."

"How can you say that, Mother? You have never been to anyplace but here, Barranquilla."

"How about me and your young brother and sister?"

15

"I promise, Mama. I'll send you money every month, as soon as I find a job."

He hugged his mother long enough, making his shirt wet from her tears. He remembered his father who was killed in an encounter with the Puerto Rican drug dealers in the middle of the Caribbean Sea. Then he hugged his small brother and sister. He could feel their bony rib cages running under his strong fingers.

He hid inside the Colombian shipping lines going to Miami via Havana, and before reaching Florida, a seaman discovered him. The captain ordered his men to throw Conrado overboard. It was already near the beach. The captain knew he could make it to the shore, and he didn't want any problem with the immigration officials. Human trafficking was a serious offense.

On his third night in Miami, he was mugged by three thugs. That was when Resty saw Conrado fighting tooth and nail, not willing to give up until his last breath. When one of the muggers pulled out a knife, that was when Resty intervened. One warning shot, and they all ran away.

He went to the severely beaten guy. "You should have just given them what they want."

"*Muchos gracias, señor,*" Conrado said.

"*De nada. Habla Ingles?*"

"*Poquito, señor.*"

Resty knew exactly what this guy was going through: an illegal immigrant, no home, no relatives, and no friends in a foreign land. There was no harm in helping this guy. "*Como se llama?*"

"Conrado."

Chapter 2
The Origins

Resty was a college professor in bio-chemistry before the government took him for a clandestine operation in the Balkans. Until he became a government operative who knew too much, he was called the Eliminator. Marked for death, he vanished like a bubble floating in the air, gone in an instant without a trace.

Any operative who tried to find him to take him out always died first in different mysterious ways. He did all the government's wet jobs (they were called wet jobs because of the blood), and he was the best. Time passed, and the Eliminator was just put in a cold case file. But the Eliminator stayed hot and was the most-sought assassin of the underworld. He had only two rules: the target should be soft, and the payment was commensurate with the target. He set those rules. He could decline, or he could accept the assignment.

A soft target was a criminal. Not easy to kill, but if he was eliminated, it was for the greater good of many. A hard target was an innocent helpless person, or a female, or a child, and he did not take any hard targets.

His finances were unlimited. He had no identity, and he was

untraceable.

He was getting old and planning to retire; last night was a twenty-three-million-dollar assignment, which almost cost him his life.

Nica was a girl with a lost identity, searching for a new world and a new identity.

She has light brown eyes, golden when illuminated, wavy, shiny brown hair, and white skin.

She was an only child. Her father was a Yugoslavian magician married to a circus contortionist acrobat from the Philippines. They met at an international circus festival in Hungary. Both were young and attractive; they fell in love and decided to get married. Graconica grew up in the circus as a child clown. She performed in different colors and faces. Running and dancing on the high wire, flying trapeze, juggling things, big and small. She traveled to many countries, spoke five languages and considered life just a game.

Her father wanted her to be the greatest magician on earth, and her mother wanted her to be the greatest acrobat dancer in the world. Her father taught her all the secrets of magic, and her mother taught her all the rituals to keep her body agile and flexible. She was not torn between these two worlds; instead, she became the combination of both of those worlds. Two became one. She became the circus alternate. She could imitate anyone in their circus team. Sometimes she was a male juggler, sometimes an acrobat, but most of the time a clown in full make-up.

She learned many cultures and could blend in easily in any community to which her parents brought her. But after the great explosion in Oklahoma City, her emotion disintegrated, and her sense of direction vanished. She lost her parents, her sense of direction, and her identity.

Chapter 3
Discovering Each Other

In the morning, Resty was in the basement gym, exercising his bandaged right arm. It was just a superficial wound by a bullet graze.

The girl came in, in a loose track suit, gently combing her hair, facing the wall of mirrors. He looked at the track suit and thought, *That's mine.* He just smiled. "Come, Nica. Stretch yourself. It's good for the body in the morning."

Nica smiled back, tucked the comb in her back pocket, and said, "Okay." She started doing her morning ritual.

Resty's jaw dropped as his eyes widened. Her way of stretching and bending was like dislocating all the bones in the body. After a few minutes of Nica's stretching and bending, he asked, "What was that?"

She looked back with a smile. "Warm-up exercise."

"That was just a warm-up? Oh my God! Nobody can do that."

"I can. My mom taught me that."

"Yes, I see that."

"Show me yours."

Resty went to the wall, picked up one of the two crossed

fencing sabers, and said, "Before my name became Resty, I won a lot of trophies and gold medals in fencing tournaments. In my younger years before I went to college, I was the fencing champion of the world." He paused, a very graceful movement of a true swordsman.

Resty continued, "Come, girl, let me teach you something useful. At least I can leave a legacy before I die."

Nica smiled and said, "If you hit me on the chest with the tip of your sword, I lose, but if I hit you on the chest with my comb, I win."

"What's the bet?" Resty asked.

"I'll tell you after I win."

"I'm going to humiliate you today, girl, to lessen your arrogance." Resty put on his most elegant stance.

She just giggled, and started running toward Resty with outstretched arms like a crucified Jesus and the comb in her right hand. Resty saw an easy target. With perfect timing, he thrust his sword toward Nica's chest. But before the tip of the sword touched her chest, she spun to her left, her chest missed the tip of the sword, but continued spinning toward her opponent, as if she was sliding through the side of the blade, and in the blink of an eye, Resty felt the comb pressed against his chest.

She looked at his eyes with a lot of energy and fun and said, "You lose."

Resty thought, *I am not just getting old. This girl is something I don't know.* "What did you win then?"

"New clothes."

"After breakfast, we'll go shopping." Resty returned the saber and continued his exercises. He could see Nica exercising also. A kind of exercise he had never seen or even heard of. But he knew the only one who could do that kind of exercise was someone who is extremely flexible, tremendously strong, and exceedingly fast.

He said to himself, *I thought that the more I see this girl, the more I will know her. But I am wrong, the more I see her the more she becomes unknown to me. What other thing shall I discover about her? Anyway she has a big heart and is willing to help anyone in need; the others are just a plus.* To him, she was just like the daughter he never had. Family life was not allowed to interfere with his kind of profession.

After they exercised, Nica pulled her hair out of the comb, knotted it, and ran to the right corner and inserted it under the carpet.

Resty said, "Hey, girl. What was that? Are you marking your territory? Or don't you know what a trash can is?"

Nica said, "No. I don't want my hair floating around the house."

At the breakfast table, Resty glanced at the headlines of the newspaper, "Circus Manager Found Cold and Hanging by a Fishing Line at the High Wire." He scanned the news and came across a line that said, "The last person who saw him alive was the boy from a nearby Hamburger Free Delivery." Resty already knew what had happened. Nothing was a coincidence in his line of thinking. Hamburger on the beach and tension marks on her arms. Resty said to himself, *Nica is a killer, almost like me.*

After breakfast, they went to the mall. She bought everything a girl needed. She thought, *At least I did not steal these. I won, and it's my prize.*

Days, weeks, and months passed. They grew fond of each other, like a real father and daughter. They discovered a lot about each other, but not their deepest secrets.

It was a sunny morning, and they were walking in the field. The smell of fresh grass and fragrant flowers was all around. Bees and butterflies flew from flower to flower. This time, both wished to let off their guards.

21

Nica started the conversation. "You never talk about your family, where you come from. I don't even know your last name."

"Resty is my only name. No first name and no family name."

"So, I will be Nica for the rest of my life?"

"No. I don't want you to be like me for the rest of your life." He sat on the grass. She sat beside him.

"I'm not getting younger. Yesterday, I told my lawyer, in case of my death or disappearance, you will inherit all that I have, except a generous gift for Conrado."

"What are you saying, Resty?"

"Your legal name is Adelin Lightston, daughter of Dresden Lightston."

"What?"

"You're intelligent enough to figure it out. My days are numbered." He paused and looked her in the eyes. "Let's go back to the house; I want you to see something."

They went to the basement. Resty went behind the rack of swords and spears, pressed the Yin and Yang sign, and it popped open. There was a digital keyboard. He typed a password and pressed his thumb for the fingerprint ID. A secret door opened along the wall of mirrors.

They entered and closed the door behind. It was a two-way mirror. The gym could be seen from the inside.

The room was a big, military workshop and laboratory combined. There were lots of tables and racks on the walls. On the right side were tables with neatly arranged weapons, repair and modification kits; on the far right was communication equipment. The left side was similar to a chemistry laboratory. Other tables consisted of several unknown items: the arsenal of a super assassin.

"The name Resty was given to me. It means Rest in Peace. Anyone I run into, he dies. Anyone who's in my way, he dies. I

22

was a government operative. I served my country with the death of many of her enemies. If I were to be caught alive by the enemy, it would be a great shame and devastation for the Agency. So, my own people tried to kill me. But I am not ready to die yet. I want to die on my own terms."

Nica asked, "The first time I saw you, those were the ones who wanted to kill you?"

"One of the many who want me dead." He walked to the communications workshop and sat on one of the high stools. "My real name was Jules Garnet, but he has already vanished into thin air. You'll never find him. Resty is a very expensive assassin with no face."

He looked at Nica and said, "I am not a bad person, it is just a matter of . . . maybe a survival instinct."

Nica looked at him and said, "Maybe it's a winner's instinct."

"I know you're just lifting my spirits."

"Why are you showing this to me?" she asked.

"Because I know someday you'll discover this room, and I don't want to leave you with a bad impression of me."

"I know that you're not a bad person."

"I'm gonna teach you how to use a gun. A person who doesn't know how to handle a gun is a very dangerous person around guns," he continued, while showing the different models and kinds of guns on the tables and racks on the wall. "These are single-shot revolvers." He picked up one handgun in each hand and spun them to show his expertise.

"Oh! You're good," Nica said.

"Don't flatter me, girl." He smiled, taking another hand gun and continued. "This is a semi-automatic. An automatic is a kind of gun that discharges several rounds in just one pressing of the trigger. A semi-automatic is just one round each."

She walked past him and went to the table with different kinds of unfamiliar weapons, and said, "I kind of like these."

"Oh, those things need a lot of practice, strength, and speed."

"Maybe you can teach me."

"Let me teach you this first." He took a handcuff and gave it to her and said, "Put it on me." He turned around and put his hands behind his back. She put the manacle on his wrist.

"First, you have to bring your hands in front." He sat down on the floor, rolled backwards, and slid his hands toward his feet, folded his knees, and his bound hands slid through in front of his feet.

"I'm sure with your flexibility, you can do it without difficulty."

He went to the table, picked up a small piece of metal and pried open the handcuff. "See! That was easy. Now, turn around with your hands on your back, and I'll teach you this simple craft."

Shaking her head, she turned around with a naughty smile, and he manacled her. She faced him, with hands together behind her, she pulled her arms upward and rotated her shoulder joints as if they had been dislocated and reduced, and she brought her arms in front. She rotated her wrists inward toward herself and slid her hands out of the manacle.

Resty was truly amazed. "What can I teach you?" he said it with a sigh and both hands spread up in the air.

Nica said, "Maybe you can teach me what you really do for a living." She put the handcuffs back on the table.

"What I do is my job, for my country and for my own survival."

"You mean killing people for money?"

"Yes and no." He picked up a metal string with rings on both ends, slid his middle fingers into each end, played with its strength as if stretching it, and continued talking. "Yes, because I actually do it. No, because every minute people die in many ways even if I don't kill them. What I mean is, no one can prevent death."

"So, you are playing death to your advantage."

"Not entirely. For me, it is not a game; it is a job. Then it is not to my advantage, but to the advantage of the one who gave me the job."

"Then you get rich in doing so."

"It is a very dangerous job." He put down the string. "At least I earn what I deserve. Look at American rock singers who just shout words accompanied by loud noises from their drums and guitars and whatever instrument they can find that produces noise, which people think is music. Then look at the American soldiers who are suffering from heat and thirst in Iraq and Afghanistan. Who earns better?"

"Rock singers don't kill; the worst they can do is just break your eardrums." She said it in a very monotonous statement without any tone of admonishment.

"What do you want to tell me, then?"

"It's a good-paying job," Nica said.

Resty looked at her and said, "And very few are qualified."

"Do you think I am qualified?" Nica asked.

He turned around. "I think you are very qualified." Balancing a dart on his forefinger, he continued. "A lot of professional killers tried to kill me; no one succeeded as you can see me now." Like a flash of lightning, he threw the dart to Nica.

Nica looked at it and caught it between her fingers.

Resty said, "But for you, you can easily kill a target." He walked to the table with a lot of electronic gadgets, transistors, and radio parts. "What I can teach you well is the power of surveillance and communications." He sat in front of a computer monitor and punched in some keys on the keyboard. "I will teach you how to emulate voices, how to divert communications so that you can't be tracked down, create dead ends, and infiltrate firewalls."

"Is this supposed to be the boring part?"

"Yes, but this will save your life. This can make you invisible. Well, not literally, but anyone who is trying to find you will never be able to locate your real position. You will have several decoys that will just go round and round in the same position."

Resty went to the large ceramic table and adjusted some flames under a funnel filled with blue liquid. "This will be your chemistry lab. You can synthesize any kind of chemical composition. For example, there are two kinds of snake venom, one is neurotoxic and the other is hematotoxic. You can produce any one of them here without actually getting the snake venom. You just produce the chemical composition here of the venom, and presto, you have it in your hands."

Nica smiled and said, "Do you want me to be a radio technician or a chemist?"

"No. I want you to be an educated Winged Viper."

"What is a Winged Viper?"

"At present time, some people call them ninjas, a Chino-Japanese concoction. Some call them assassins from a European broken Arabic. But those terms are so limited. Ninjas and assassins are trained, but a Winged Viper is born."

"Can you tell me something I understand?"

"Yes. Anybody can be a karate black belt, but not anybody can be a boxer. To be a boxer, one should be born with the strength, stamina, agility, and speed of a boxer; then he can train to be a boxer. It is something called in-born. Yours is in-born."

"It's a good story; it makes me feel sleepy. So, a Winged Viper is a human then?"

"No. According to the legend, the original Winged Viper was a snake, born every millennium. The tip of its tail is deadlier than the scorpion. It has four razor-sharp poisoned horns, two on top of its head and one on each side. It is impossible to hold it on its head the way you catch a snake. It attacks whomever it likes, big or small, even without provocation, with no fear or mercy. The tips of its tongues are as sharp and as deadly as its fangs. The tips of its wings have claws that grab and paralyze its prey. Its skin is covered with double-edged razor-sharp scales that cut in any direction."

"So, a Winged Viper is a snake."

"No. History tells us about the Winged Viper. Every one thousand years, a Winged Viper is born; they become legends of their time. The Bible has many Winged Vipers. Genesis chapter six, verses one to four talk of the inbreeding of gods and humans, which became the heroes of old, men of fame. One of them is called Samson, who in these times would be branded a terrorist, or suicide bomber. The Greeks had a legend about a Winged Viper in the time of their ancestors. They named him Hercules. In the legend, he was a son of God from a human mother."

"I was never right."

"We'll get into that. Then you'll never be wrong."

Resty walked back and picked up a handgun. "I am going to teach you how to use a gun, aim accurately, and zero in on your target."

"Yes, sir." Playfully executing a snappy salute to his direction, she thought, *He will teach me to be a better killer.* She noticed that Resty was again staring at her diamond-studded pendant, as he used to do. Her mind went to her past, memories of her travel before reaching California.

She remembered when she hitched a ride in a dirty, old Chevy van. She had slept for a while. When she woke up, she was already bound, hands and feet. She felt the van stop. The door of the van opened. Two guys bent over, covering the moonlight from her view and producing two silhouettes of ape-like creatures. One pulled her by the legs, and the other lifted her like a rug, for she was so small and light. She did not move. Instead, she studied the surroundings and found out that nothing was familiar. It was dark, but the surroundings were illuminated by the moon and cloudless sky. She was brought into an old house, dragged down the stairs into a dark, pungent, wet, and cold basement. She could not recognize the smell, but it smelled bad. She thought it was the smell of a rotting animal, but it was a little bit sweet and salty to the tongue. Her salivation increased and she wanted to vomit, but she just let her saliva drool out from her mouth.

The bulky guy just placed her on top of a wooden table. Beside her were a wooden chopping board, a big stained metal basin, and a small ax. The guys went out and closed the door behind them. Nica heard the door lock, and then she heard a chain being connected; she guessed it was a padlock to double-lock their catch.

She was inside the house of the cannibalistic, mentally deranged family who terrified the nation with their ways of killing and eating their victims. But Nica did not know anything about them.

Inside the house, the old lady asked, "D'you guys catcha sunthin?"

The big guy said, "Yah. Buh t'was too small. No mea' a'rowl."

"T'will be a gooh soup. Is't young?"

"Jah. Jhe's young. I dink so."

"Yow uncle and yow brother showd be here any minute now with a catcha. I saw them follow a buncha' young boys and girls in their convertible."

The lady went to the steaming, big pot, stirred it a bit, and tasted it. "Yum. Taste gooh."

The two guys slumped on the sofa. The bulky guy kept picking his teeth. The tall and thin guy crossed his right leg and started picking his toes and smelled his fingers every time he picked something.

The sound of an engine could be heard getting louder and louder until it stopped. The lady said, "They cowd be it now."

The voice from outside was like an animal growl, "I go' one still alive here. Three are ready for jhopping. We din't able to save the blood, they keep on crawling away."

The two guys got up from the sofa and went outside to help the new arrivals carry the load of dead bodies.

The lady said, "Ge'ra live one together with that small catcha in the basement."

Nica already adjusted her eyes to the darkness. She kept her position. She was already free but pretended still to be bound. She heard the heavy footsteps of the bulky guy, dragging something heavy. She heard the opening of the padlock, then the clanking of the chains, and then the door lock. The door opened but did not reveal any brightness, instead the shadow of the ape-like creature holding a moaning creature by the waist. The bulky guy came down the stairs carrying the barely alive catch. The victim's feet thudded on every step of the stairs. Nica thought, "This one is still alive."

The bulky guy placed the victim next to Nica. That was when Nica sprang from the table and somersaulted to the floor. She wanted to see what this giant would do next. The hulk went to the wall and picked up the chainsaw. He pulled the starter, and the deafening engine sound roared inside the basement. Nica picked up the ax from the table. She had perfected the use of an ax in the circus performance. The hulk was just an easy target. She threw the ax straight to his forehead. The sound was more of a thud. The hulk growled in pain. He took the ax out, leaving the gap on his forehead bleeding. He just threw away the ax as if nothing had happened. He was still coming after Nica. Nica knew that this guy would never just die. He should be decapitated and cooked. She stood still, so that the hulk would have a perfect aim on her. He ran toward her, with raised arms, aiming the electric saw toward Nica. Just before the electric saw came crashing on her, she twisted to her left, the electric saw missing her, she got hold of the hulk's arm and used the guy's strength on his own forward and downward momentum, she twisted his arms toward himself, aiming for the legs. The electric saw went straight on both legs, amputating them instantly. He released the electric saw in pain and panic. Nica saw her chance. She took the electric saw and immediately aimed for the guy's arms and then his neck, and then she turned off the electric saw and gently placed it on the floor.

She went to attend to the other victim. "Hey. Wake up. You have to wake up." She was a young girl, maybe in her late teens. Nica was desperate to wake her up. "What's your name?"

The girl answered in a lethargic voice, "Ellen. Ellen Smith."

"Ellen. You have to wake up, or we won't be able to escape from these crazy people."

"What do you want me to do?"

"I need you to stand, jump a little several times, and shake yourself."

She did as she was instructed. "All my body aches."

"Ignore the pain, or else you die."

Ellen was trying to wake herself up. With the fear of terrible death, her adrenaline started to kick in. "Yes. What shall we do?"

"Just follow behind me. When I tell you to run, run as fast as you can and never look back."

"You saved my life. But what if I don't see you again?"

"Never mind. Forget me."

"No! How can I?" She took off her gold necklace with a *diamond-studded, gold, flower pendant. "Take this. Whenever our road crosses again, show me this necklace, and I will remember you."* Nica took and wore it around her small neck. She took the

30

two-foot hatchet hanging on the wall. She could juggle seven hatchets like this one. In the circus, she had mastered the use of bladed weapons, in case someone was sick and needed an alternate.

Nica remembered shouting at Ellen to run as fast as she could and never look back, after she decapitated the tall, thin guy who was guarding the door. The next thing that happened was the necessary thing for her to do. Cut them all to pieces and cook them. Then she continued to California.

She touched the diamond-studded pendant and remembered to go ahead and take the gun.

Chapter 4
Educating the Winged Viper

The lesson began. Day by day, Nica was increasing in knowledge and skills. At night, she read. Every week, Resty reversed the process until Nica had no more sensation of day or night. She could sleep anytime she wanted. Her biological clock of breakfast or suppertime did not exist anymore. Food for nutrition was what mattered.

Some of her training was done blindfolded in pitch darkness. She learned the different smells of things, their difference in smell when they are wet, dry, or hot. She learned to weigh things in her hands. She could tell if the gun was loaded or not, or how many rounds were still remaining just by holding it in her hand. She could hear the sound and locate a cockroach crawling on the wall.

For many days, they went to shopping centers, all kinds of stores, looking at different kinds of shoes, clothes for men and women, and even to the stores that sell used goods and clothing.

Once a week, they drove in a random direction for one hour, parked somewhere, and then walked in a random direction for two hours, then back to the house. They would make a list of five characters seen while driving and another five persons seen while walking. Nica would describe those subjects from head to toe, the style of their clothes and where they had been bought, whether brand-new or used, mannerisms, economic and educational background, habit, and everything she could tell about that person and the reasons why. On the remaining six days, Nica was able to locate the house, work, or school of those ten people. Sometimes posing as a salesperson, she was able to interview some of them to verify her previous theories about that person. On the sixth week, she almost got a perfect score. She had a wrong impression of a guy who was a deeply hidden gay, who went daily to the gym building his muscles.

She learned how to play the piano and learned ballroom dancing. Her hidden life made her confident, strong, and humble.

Four years passed.

By the time she finished the course, she was a completely educated Winged Viper. Then in the middle of the night, the coded telephone rang and then died out. Resty looked at the number, went out of the house, and drove for twenty minutes to a public pay phone
and dialed the number.

Resty put a gadget on the mouthpiece and said, "Do you need my services?"

"Joe Hernandes, Mexican arms dealer. Based in Crenshaw and Adams . . ."

After the conversation, he hung up and turned around. He was startled. In front of him was Nica with a wide smile.

Nica said, "So, that was a deal?"

"What are you doing here? How did you come here? Oh my God, Nica. My child, your surprises never end." He was sure Nica had overheard the conversation about the elimination of a certain target.

They went back to the car, and Resty drove at a leisurely pace.

"Let's do it," Nica said excitedly.

"No!"

"It's up to you. I'm just offering a hand."

On their drive home, Resty asked, "So, how did you follow me? Don't tell me you ran?"

"No, I didn't. I was behind you all the time, in your blind spot, from the time that coded telephone rang."

Nica looked around and said, "Hey! You're lost; this is not the way home."

"I know. But I am not lost. This is exactly where I want to go. I will study the vicinities of my target: escape routes, possible traps, and the habit of that place." They turned left, and Resty continued. "Once I have identified my target, I am the only one who knows when, where, and how, minimizing the success of a trap and maximizing the target's vulnerability."

"And you have to do it right now?"

"Yes. In this way, I can be familiar with the surroundings at the earliest possible time. Then if they put up a trap, it will be easy to spot. There will be changes from the first time I saw it." He slowed down. "Look at the rooftops, see how many have dish antennas, how many windows have curtains and blinds, how many corners have trash bins, be familiar with the surroundings now, then see the difference tomorrow, then presto, you will see your traps. You should always be one step ahead of them."

"Then attack your target in the most unexpected place and time," Nica said.

"That is one way to do it," Resty said.

"Is there any other way?" Nica asked.

"There are endless ways of taking out your target."

"Who's your target?"

"Joe Hernandes, an ex-cop who is now an arms dealer. He was a dirty cop, that's why he was dishonorably discharged."

"Who ordered it?"

"Learn the secret of the trade. Pretend that you don't know and you don't care who ordered it."

"What if he did not pay you?"

"Take him as your target as quickly as possible."

"Do you really know who ordered it and why?"

"As to who, yes, but as to why, I suspect that my target has been under surveillance for some time now, and my client will be exposed if Joe is caught alive. He could be somebody high in the government with some military connections. So, my target should be eliminated as quickly as possible."

"Your target is under surveillance, so he is already inside the trap, and you want to go with him inside the trap?"

"This is my last job, and then I'll retire. I'll vanish for a while till all things cool down."

"You might be caught or even killed in your last job. There is a saying; the last is always the hardest," Nica said in a very plain, unemotional tone.

"It adds to the thrill," Resty said with a smile. "One important part of the trade is to not get caught. If you can't do that, don't get caught alive. But then if still you can't do that, and you are caught, try your very best not to be seriously injured. Save yourself for later, to fight back and then escape.

"You should be alert and focused on what is in front of you and everything within your visual field; but you must be ten times more alert about what is behind you and what is not within your visual field because that's the one that can harm you."

After two weeks of surveillance, Resty made the plan. He would take the target at three in the morning. That was the time when the target would finish his work in the old warehouse, go to his car, and then go home, with at least two more cars of his bodyguards.

It was dark and cold and humid. A smell of death was impending in the atmosphere.

Resty was on top of a five-story building next to the warehouse where Joe Hernandes was supposed to come out in a few minutes. A span of a short time-frame of thirty seconds was all Resty needed to take out the target. He would use a medium-range, small sniper rifle. The target was not that far, and the trajectory was downward. He did not see any problem in the situation. It was too easy.

At this time and place, darkness was his friend. The head was the prime target of a sharpshooter. He did not prefer the body, because his target might be wearing a bulletproof vest. The head was always his identifying mark. He positioned himself. Wearing a black nylon suit, without movement, he was just an invisible speck on top of the roof, waiting patiently. At exactly seven minutes past three in the cold morning, his target, Joe Hernandes, emerged from the big door of the warehouse, surrounded by his six bodyguards. Resty pointed his rifle directly at the head of Joe Hernandes. He counted. He should be able to pull the trigger within the span of thirty seconds. He began counting and positioning, looking for the best open shot. When he reached ten, an extremely bright light blinded him. He was surrounded by bright lights positioned around him from the spotlights on top along the sides and corners of the very building he was standing on.

At this split-second, he realized that this had been a trap from the very start of the phone call. After the phone call, he toured the place and noticed the dark, unlit, big spotlights on several buildings. Those buildings were the possible positions that a sniper may choose.

Two choppers with blinding spotlights focused on him. With deafening voice, the sound of the megaphone was just like a dream to Resty.

"Do not move. You are completely surrounded. We will open fire if you try to move an inch." He did not even breathe.

His mind raced. He thought, *I am caught. Surely this will be a big-time torture before they finally throw my unidentified corpse to the sea. Either I will be partly or eaten whole by the sea creatures, or I will be washed offshore, or both.* A lot of questions and uncertainties raced through his mind. He thought, *What will happen to Nica? She can take care of herself, I suppose. How about Conrado? His family is waiting for him.* Then he looked up to the sky full of tiny dots. He thought, *Oh my God. I did not expect my life to end this way.*

Suddenly the tiny dots in the sky became sparkling bright spots. He thought, *Those are stars.* Suddenly, he heard an explosion mixed with a lot of gunfire, but still he could not move. Everything was mixed up at the same time, all the electricity was off for four city blocks around him and the choppers losing their focus, too, collided and exploded in midair. Then there was total darkness, except for the blasting fire going down with the choppers.

Something caught him on the waist and pulled him down the wall of the building. He looked behind him and saw the hooded face of Nica a few inches from his own, with a naughty smile. Within the span of not more than three seconds, they were down the building and quickly went inside a black, sleek, sports car and sped off down the road. In a few minutes, they blended into the traffic flow of Western Avenue and then Freeway 10.

Resty asked Nica, "How did you do it?"

"When we went on the tour of the area after your phone call, I saw the big spotlights on top of several buildings. Then I thought to myself, if those spotlights were to be turned on, you would be like a sitting duck. But I saw the transformer that supplies power to all those buildings. I took it out with a little explosion, just to disable it, and then there was darkness. I tangled the two choppers with the use of a long, steel cable that I shot in the air, hoping that each end would be caught by their propellers. It worked."

Resty looked at her and said, "No. I mean those dead people."

Nica said, "Oh, you mean your target? He was taken out along with others who were trying to protect him." She continued, "They were very close to me after the darkness. I just shot them on my way up when I got you down."

The next morning, the breaking news of the explosion and gunfire in Crenshaw and Adams, stated, ". . . Joe Hernandes and four of his associates were killed in what appeared to be gang-related activities leaving others injured . . . "

Resty said, "I will go somewhere. Maybe vanish forever. You know, they know me."

Part II

"Death of one person can be paid but once."
~Shakespeare, *Anthony and Cleopatra*

Chapter 1
The Call

With bitter tears welling out from her eyes, the little girl watched her father hanged. His bulging eyes, his protruding tongue, his extremely red swollen face, and the spastic jerk of his slow agonizing death will never be erased from her memory.

It is payback time; I am now in the position to make them pay. She had the phone number given by her own personal secret service that just came from South America, with simple instructions on how to call the hired killer.

"Madam Bint Basheer, this one is very reliable. No identity and no identity requirement, just money."

"You can leave me now, Hassan." She bid him goodbye and dialed the number. The first was a single ring, and then an electronic voice message. *The number you dialed is not a working number.* She dialed a second time, another electronic message. *We're sorry, the number is not complete as dialed, please check the number and dial again.* She dialed a third time. There was a long dial tone, and then it went dead. The fourth time she dialed, the phone rang.

"What can I do for you?"

She said, "I want a plane crashed this week."

The person at the other end asked, "And who could be on that plane?"

She said bitterly, "The people who hanged my father. Monday, Flight Six-Two-Four, Islamabad."

"Twenty-million dollars, cash." The voice was as cold as ice.

"Do you want it in advance?" she asked.

"Half of it now and half after." He gave the details on how to arrange the payment.

"Deal." She agreed. It was a lazy Saturday night. She was a rich and powerful client. On this warm summer night, she was refreshing herself on the rooftop of her mansion under the moonless sky, a tepid breeze blowing her long, flowing hair away from her beautiful face. The long-awaited moment of her vengeance was almost at hand.

Monday, 10:00 p.m.: She was in front of her seventy-two-inch flat-screen TV.

"Breaking News: *The president with his top military and religious advisers including an American diplomat was killed in a tragic plane crash minutes ago. The investigation is ongoing . . .*"

She was still watching the news when her private phone rang. "Ahlo?"

"The other half is due in twenty minutes. Black bag, table six, Carl's Jr., the corner of Sixth and Virgil." The line went dead, and she turned off the TV, with a triumphant smile.

A week later, in another part of the globe:

General Silversmith held his throat, heaved his last, dropped to the floor, still warm but dead. Three seconds after he answered the secure red phone in his private room that nobody could touch.

It was on the Breaking News.

His death cost a total of sixteen million dollars for the señor.

The phone rang, and the señor answered, "Hola?"

"Señor Alejandro, the job is done. My bag is waiting for the other half of the sixteen."

Señor Alejandro said, "It will be there right away." He was so perplexed and terrified that this killer even addressed him by name, like a common acquaintance. He thought, *I think this is his way of scaring his clients into paying. He is good. Nobody is supposed to know who I am.*

He put down the phone and yelled, "Sebastian, get the money and take it yourself, I repeat, yourself."

Señor Alejandro was the Colombian cocaine supplier of the Americas. One of his fleet had been busted by General Silversmith.

Three days later, in the LAPD Forensic Laboratory, Dr. Yokohama had just finished with the red phone taken from General Silversmith's office.

Dr. Yokohama shouted, "Bryanna! Don't turn off the radio; my program is coming on in a minute." Then he faced the LAPD detectives and said, "It was one of the deadliest poisons I have ever seen in my career. Once it touches the skin, you have three seconds to ask for forgiveness for your sins."

Detective Mark Fielder said, "Doctor, I don't have time for your riddles."

"The one that killed the general is a poison similar to the poisonous frog of the rainforest of South America, *Phyllobates terribilis*," the doctor said.

"Do I start in Brazil?" Detective Fielder said.

"No, no, no," Dr. Yokohama said. "What I said is *similar,*" he said, raising his hands using the second and middle fingers to make the sign of quotation marks on the word similar.

"The poison from the poison frog of South America does not permeate the skin, but if it is on the tip of an arrow, you're gone in an instant. This one is chemically, maybe genetically altered to permeate the skin."

Detective Fielder said, "I got more than enough. Thank you, doctor." He started walking toward the door.

Dr. Yokohama yelled to the detective, "Wait! I haven't told you that the poison was smeared on the earpiece to make sure that nobody would be killed accidentally . . ."

Detective Fielder turned. "Doctor, I don't care. For me, it's enough that it was murder, not a natural death."

As a student, Detective Mark Fielder had been a ferocious football player, which made it possible for him to finish college. In his career, he never stopped until his case was solved. Very few were unsolved. The case of General Silversmith was just another assignment to be solved. The detective's first question was: Who benefited the most in the general's death? The second would be, of course: Who carried out the assassination?

His partner was Detective Jamila Amin, a brilliant graduate of the L.A. Police Academy. She was a descendant of a long line of Arab police detectives in the Middle East. Her father took her to America when he was posing as an ordinary tourist while following an international terrorist. That was when Jamila was attracted to the American lifestyle. She persuaded her father to let her study in America, and finally became a U.S. citizen.

Captain Montero gave the introductions: "Detective Mark Fielder, this is Detective Jamila Amin. You will be working together in finding whoever killed General Silversmith."

"My partner is a woman?" Detective Fielder faced the police captain. "Last time was a punk, now a woman?"

The captain said, "Prejudice will not be tolerated in my office."

Detective Fielder raised his arms and said, "Oh my God! Captain Montero, do you know who my suspect is? Do you know that this assignment will be extremely dangerous?"

Detective Amin intervened. "Don't worry about me, Detective Fielder. My father was a police detective, and I've seen him survive a lot of cases far more dangerous than this one."

Detective Fielder faced Detective Amin. "Detective, just because your father was a good police detective and a survivor doesn't mean that you will be, too."

Detective Amin said, "Of course not. But I learned a lot from him even before I went to school in America."

"Okay, let's get down to business." Detective Fielder gave up. "What's the plan?" he asked. "How about the one who hired the assassin?"

Captain Montero said, "That subject is for me. For now, worry about yours first."

Detective Amin interjected. "Captain, why is it so important to you to unmask this assassin?"

"Because," Captain Montero paused. "He could be the key to other international assassinations across the globe. This one is unstoppable and unidentifiable. He works strictly for money and nothing else. At least that was what that FBI guy told me. He is following the money trail, and it always ends at the same point before the trail disappears."

"Where does the money trail end?" Detective Amin asked.

"It's like this. There will be a large cash withdrawal in dollars somewhere around the globe, and then there will be a mysterious death of an important character, then another equal cash withdrawal from somewhere, again in dollars. It appears that half before and half after is the deal. Then that's it. Nobody knows where the money goes; it just vanishes like bubbles."

Detective Fielder said, "So, money is the best bait. That's easy."

Chapter 2
Mafiosi versus Yakuza

Don Victorini was fuming in anger. "Salvador! How much did we lose to the *Japones* this last deal? Don't answer me! You know it, don't you? It's thirty million dollars, *coño*."

Salvador was trembling in fear. "Yes, Don Victorini."

"Yes! Yes, yes, yes, Don Victorini. You are only good for yes." Don Victorini was thinking. "Do you have any solution to this problem? Don't answer me! I know you will say yes. Then what is it?"

"Don Victorini," Salvador was becoming bright-eyed now, "I know of somebody who can eliminate our problem, but he is expensive."

"How much?" Don Victorini yelled.

"Twenty million dollars," Salvador said, trembling again.

"Call him and make the deal," Don Victorini said, "and I want it as soon as possible."

Chapter 3
The Deal

Salvador dialed the number. The first was a single ring and then an electronic voice message: *The number you dialed is not a working number.* He dialed a second time. Another electronic message: *We're sorry, the number is not complete as dialed, please check the number and dial again.* He dialed a third time, there was a long dial tone, and then it went dead. The fourth time he dialed, the phone rang three times, then an electronic message: *Leave your name and phone number, and I will call you back as soon as I can.*

An hour later, in a phone booth on a busy street, Resty put a tiny gadget on the mouthpiece and dialed the number. Salvador picked up the phone and answered angrily, "*Bueno*? Don's residence."

An electrifying voice spoke. "Do you need my services?"

Salvador gasped. He thought his heart had stopped. He said to himself, *My God, the angel of Death!*

Salvador answered, "Yes, I do." He was extremely terrified just hearing the sound from the other end, a far greater fear than what he felt for Don Victorini.

Salvador gave the target. "They will be at the penthouse. Six persons, all are the heads of each yakuza clan. Guarded by twenty-four notorious killers, called ninjas."

"Mister Salvador," Resty said over the phone, "your wife's name is Linda, and your daughter is Harmonica. Would you kill them for twenty million dollars?"

"No!" Salvador almost shouted in fear. Inside his mind was pure terror. He thought, *He even knows my wife's and kid's names. Undoubtedly, he also knows my home address.*

Resty, almost whispering now, said, "You want me to kill a total of thirty persons for twenty million dollars? And . . . don't forget, they are not that easy to kill."

Salvador knew that the assassin just wanted a raise, and he knew for him they are an easy target.

Don Victorini, who was listening from the other end, signaled forty.

Salvador, now in a convincing voice like a perfect salesman, said, "Forty million then?"

"Now, tell me, who are the targets? After I eliminated the six, do you want me to also eliminate the other twenty-four?"

Don Victorini smelled another increase. He signaled no, the six was enough for the deal.

Salvador said, "The six are enough, but I think you can only reach the six over their dead bodies." Salvador sounded like he was trying to scare the killer.

"That's why the don's paying me, right?" Resty said.

"Of course," Salvador agreed with a frightened voice that he could barely hide.

"We talk only in cash. Take it personally in a black bag, it is only twenty kilos . . ." Resty gave the address, hung up, and left.

Chapter 4
At the Yakuza HQ

Hiroyuki was expertly arranging his *shuriken*, the throwing stars that had just been soaked in poison. Each one was dangerous and deadly sharp. The hand of the thrower might be injured if he was not an expert in holding this deadly instrument. Hiroyuki had mastered its use in childhood. He still remembered his master in Kyoto, a brutal killer who knew no mercy. The first throw would be to the forehead, the second to the neck, and the third just below the sternum. All were deadly. The first three throws landed on the target in less than half a second. This was what he had mastered as a ninja. He could take out three targets in just one throw. Besides this skill, his sense of smell was like that of a trained dog; his ears were as sharp, too. Even if he was sleeping, a tiny unusual sound awakened him, flaring his nose to analyze what it could be. It was now just an automatic reflex embedded in his system. These were the things that kept him alive, and the reason why he was one of the twenty-four elite guards of the yakuza leaders.

He stepped out of the training room. On his first step out, he smelled something different. It was a good smell, but it did not belong here. He signaled to Koizumi that something strange was just around.

Koizumi was a dart master. He could hit a fly moving in the air with a deadly dart. He was a very strict disciplinarian. Only the two of them were left on the second floor, the training room. The others had left five minutes ago to go to the first floor, which looked like a normal living room with a dining area in the right corner.

The first floor served as the first stop when someone wanted to meet with the leaders. There was a small hallway to the elevator; the right side wall was a two-way mirror with an x-ray, monitored by security men in the basement. Once they saw an imminent danger, the guest would be stopped on the second floor, where the danger would be neutralized, or killed if necessary.

The third floor was the conference room, for guests or otherwise. No one was allowed up to the fourth floor except for the six *oyabuns* of the yakuza; it was like a sacred place to them. The *oyabuns* were the fathers of the six largest yakuza clans in Japan.

From the far wall of the hallway, a stranger in black appeared in a slightly loose, black coverall, intentionally catching the ninja's attention. Hiroyuki was quick in throwing his *shuriken* at the target, followed by Koizumi with his darts. But the stranger was holding a wooden board, one foot square, one inch thick, which he used to catch the whizzing stars and darts. In a swift dancing motion, he moved toward them.

Resty was so smooth in the gracefulness of his movements; his left hand was very precise in catching the moving instruments of death. The two ninjas saw everything, and as if in just a blink of an eye, two throwing stars seem to bounce back at them coming from the right hand of the stranger after he picked them out of the board. It was as if the stars were caught before they even landed on the board, in a very swift and gentle motion, which the ninjas did not have even the time to move away from, because when they saw the object, it was already between their eyes. It was almost painless. The poison of the *shuriken* was so potent that the time between being hit and feeling its pain was cut in half. All was blindingly bright and then nothingness.

Resty moved swiftly and untied the waist scarf from the ninja where the remaining *shuriken* were. Resty also took the darts from the other ninja and told himself, *These might be useful just in case.* He also took two smoke balls from the ninja.

Like a swift, soundless, running cat, he moved toward the door going to the third floor, where the six *oyabuns* were holding their meeting.

Nobutaka was a highly respected *oyabun*. He was not only the oldest among them, but his ancestors were also the founding *oyabuns* of this organization.

Nobutaka had an early ticket back to Tokyo, where his lovely three-year-old granddaughter was waiting for him. He had promised her a dancing and talking Dora, which he bought in the local Chinatown. He told his son-in-law, "I want her to be spoiled, more spoiled than her mother. I want her to grow thinking that nothing in this world is beyond her reach."

Huro said, "Father, it will be difficult for me to —"

"Don't bother," Nobutaka interrupted. "As long as I'm alive, I'll make sure that she gets what she wants."

He was happy and smiling at the pleasant memory. The other *oyabuns* thought that he was in good spirits because they had been successful in overcoming the don of the street, with a profit of over twenty million dollars. Drugs were a good business.

It was at that sudden moment when a stranger appeared at the door, throwing two smoke balls with an instant blindness and the smell of the drug they were dealing with was just a fleeting moment.

Nobutaka saw the sudden clouds; a sharp thing pierced his

throat, memories of Omaya, his granddaughter, playing in the park, tightness in his lungs gripped his whole body toward the center, and then he saw nothing, memories gone forever.

The next day...

The events were in the newspapers not as murders but as natural deaths, and funeral ceremonies were held without bodies, just jars of ashes of the cremated *oyabuns*.

The successors were crying from anger, their hearts bleeding for vengeance. They knew exactly who did this to them, although there was no evidence, and no answer how it was done and by whom.

But Detectives Mark Fielder and Jamila Amin wondered, *How could six prominent Japanese businessmen with their two associates die at the same time, be cremated at the same time?* The two were sent to Japan and the six remained here for funeral services, but not to be buried, just displayed and mourned. They smelled something unusual, and it seemed connected with their assignment.

In their own analysis of the investigation, that building was impenetrable from all angles. The first floor, which was the only way up, was heavily guarded although it looked normal. The fourth floor had only one entry. Inside was a highly ornamented floor with six large rooms, simple and comfortable, but one could feel this was a royal place of retreat, very conducive for contemplation or other secluded and intimate activities.

Detective Amin concluded that they could have been killed on the third floor, during a meeting or a similar gathering.

The other two men served as guards, and were killed, of course, to have access to the third floor. There was no direct evidence; this was all educated speculation. Detective Jamila Amin thought she was right, and Detective Mark Fielder could only agree, because he had arrived at the same conclusion, only his was that the two were just incidental targets.

Chapter 5
Two Inventions of Dr. Yokohama:
Eye of the Eagle and the Golden Eye

Dr. Yokohama was sitting in a revolving easy chair while explaining, "I can find anyone on Earth within twenty-four hours. The only thing that I will require is a sample from that person, something that I can use to build up a DNA ID. I am renting a small section from a satellite service. During a single rotation of the Earth, my program will scan every inch of the Earth up to five thousand feet above and below the Earth's surface. Once the program finds the DNA match, it will lock in, and it will remain locked wherever the subject goes. When I get enough funding, I will be able to finance my own satellite, which will move opposite the Earth's direction at the same speed, so the twenty-four hours will become twelve hours, until I develop a high-speed satellite that can scan the whole Earth in six hours. And this I call, 'Eye of the Eagle.' Yes, I can find the person that you are searching for."

Dr. Yokohama continued, "My second invention is an implantable device. It is a transparent, microscopic, three-D radio-camera, with reception to any cell site, as in any cellular phone. Then if the site is out of range, it will automatically be covered by the satellite, as in any satellite phone, with GPS embedded in the camera. Many crimes and other mysteries will be gone forever."

The doctor paused. "It will be implanted between the cornea and the iris, for a wider visual field and so that the person who is wearing it will not be distracted during his sleep, because the vision is superficial. It will not pass through the lens or the retina, where the brain interprets the vision through the optic nerve. The wearer does not actually control it. If it is implanted in a newborn, he will grow up without knowing that he has one."

The doctor shifted to his right. "It has two added special features: x-ray vision and night vision. Even if the person with an implanted device was blindfolded or the eyes were closed, or even in pitch darkness inside a cave, the monitoring system can continuously see what is in the visual field of the Golden Eye. And remember, the focus is digital the one who is monitoring it can take a close-up view of a vehicle's plate number five miles away in total darkness with the clarity of the summer sun at noon."

The doctor faced them. "I am trying a way to connect this to the optic nerve so that in the future the wearer will be able to control its functions."

Dr. Yokohama was a full-time, civilian employee of the LAPD as a forensic pathologist. His private practice was his part-time job —actually his passion—inventions for the future.

The doctor stood up. He was short, probably an inch taller than a midget. He said, "Do these things sound good to you, detectives?"

"Yes, of course," answered Detective Fielder, still mesmerized by what he had heard.

"Come to my laboratory. I'll introduce you to my assistant, and you may see for yourselves the prototype and how it really works."

They entered Dr. Yokohama's private laboratory, and the

doctor introduced them to his assistant. "Bryanna, this is Detective Mark Fielder and Detective Jamila Amin. They want to see our project."

Bryanna Johanson was a former student of Dr. Yokohama. She was dedicated to her work, introverted, young, and full of energy.

Detective Amin took a small glass tube out of her pocket and said, "Doctor Yokohama, maybe you can locate where this is from."

The doctor took it and said, "I'll see what I can do." He handed it to Bryanna.

"What is it and where did you get that?" Detective Fielder whispered in her ear.

"Just a long shot. I scraped it from the rug of General Silversmith; maybe nothing," Detective Jamila answered, shrugging her shoulders.

Detective Fielder, holding in his fingertips a strand of brown, short hair, showed it, and said, "How about this, Doctor?"

The doctor took it and carefully pressed it between two glass slides and said, "I hope this is not evidence. Or else you'll be breaking protocols." He handed it to Bryanna.

"No, it is not. It's just to see how far your experiment will go." Detective Fielder stopped and asked, "By the way doctor, where did you get all the funding for these?"

"Oh yes, from the County thru the Griffith Observatory."

After the tour of Dr. Yokohama's laboratory, the detectives were quietly walking outside toward their car in the parking lot, not knowing what to say. Behind them was the amber sky, the setting sun being blocked by the doctor's office.

The doctor bid them goodbye and said, "I'll call you both tomorrow with the results."

Inside the car, Detective Jamila Amin, looking far ahead, said, "You're good." Then she turned her face toward Detective Mark

Fielder. "Finding a strand of hair that could be the killer's hair."

"No. If that's your reason, then I am not because that's the hair of Buddy, my mastiff. Just testing the doctor's invention." Detective Mark Fielder was smiling now.

Detective Amin looked far ahead again and said, "You're mean."

The next day, at Detective Mark Fielder's office.

The phone rang. Mark picked it up. "Hello?"

"Hello. Good afternoon. This is Doctor Yokohama. I found your subject, the origin of the hair strand. At first they were two moving objects, one in small circles and the other in bigger circles. Then the objects became subjects, the first was a dog, which I believe is in your house, the second is your jacket, which is not moving now. I think it is hanging somewhere in your office."

Detective Fielder said, "Uhhuuum?" That was all he could answer.

The doctor continued. "And please tell Detective Amin that her sample came from the ceiling of the general's office. In case I may be of further help to you, please feel free to come by. Goodbye and have a good day."

"Thank you, Doctor." Those were the only words that could come out of Detective Fielder's mouth.

Detective Amin put out her tongue and pulled down her lower eyelids and said, "Bleeeh! Good for you."

Detective Fielder, with his index finger raised, replied, "No! No, no, no. My point is, we can really use the doctor."

Detective Fielder faced Detective Amin and said, "I think we should check the second and third floors of the yakuza headquarters again. Do you think we missed something?"

Detective Amin sat down on the sofa, put the pen between her teeth, slightly biting it, and said, "Do you really think that the killer might accidentally have left a strand of falling hair or dandruff on their floor? I don't think so!"

Detective Fielder stood up. "Why? Do you have a better idea?"

Detective Amin took out the pen from her mouth. "Yes! I think I have."

"Then tell me!" Detective Fielder started to pace the room, like a hungry predator.

Teasing, Detective Amin replied, "No! I will not tell you." She stood up, picked up her bag and coat, heading toward the door, and said, "We are going to do it, and we will get dirty doing it. So follow me, and we'll start getting dirty."

Detective Fielder took out his mastiff-fur-covered jacket and followed Detective Amin.

The next day before sundown. At the Don's mansion.

"Salvador! Go to the marina and prepare the yacht. I am going to Catalina," Don Victorini shouted.

"Yes, Don Victorini, right away, Don." Like a dog with his tail tucked under, Salvador left the room.

Outside the don's mansion, a black van with tinted glass was parked at a discreet corner under the shade of a tree, unnoticed by any passersby, and inside were four Arabs waiting for Salvador's brand-new, red Corvette.

The giant, electronic gate opened, Salvador's car emerged, and the gate closed behind. Before the car gained speed, a stooped, hooded figure, walking very slowly, crossed the street, blocking Salvador's path.

The black van followed behind. Salvador opened the window, put out an arm, and started to shout at the hooded figure. But the hooded figure jumped toward Salvador, followed by two others from the black van, and yanked Salvador out. The hooded figure went inside the Corvette and sped away, while Salvador was pushed inside the black van.

Salvador was bleeding from the mouth. Nobody was talking now, not even a slight sound. Every time Salvador tried to talk or even make a slight sound, someone slapped him on his face. The effect of what they were doing to him was now terrifying. Salvador knew they were some kind of kidnappers for ransom or whatever, he didn't know, but they could kill him anytime they wanted, and he was not ready to die yet. His little *Bonita* was waiting for him for her fifth birthday party. He had promised his daughter that the first thing she would see tomorrow at sunrise would be her pappy, ready to decorate the yard for the children's party. She had invited all her kindergarten classmates, teachers, and their friends and neighbors.

No talking, no moaning; he just quietly trembled in fear.

The van stopped, Salvador was blindfolded, violently yanked out of the van, and somebody loudly slapped him on his shoulder. The sudden loud sound was frightening; it made him jerk in a spasm, with the kind of fear that crawled through all his flesh, made all his skin damp and hairs stand up. He could feel that they had entered an enclosure, maybe a room or a warehouse; it felt cold and damp. He was pushed down on a wet floor. Still nobody was talking. He could hear a faint sound from somewhere. The sound of a weak and tired scream could be heard coming nearer and nearer. He was lying on the ground in the fetal position; he opened his eyes and peeked under the blindfold. He was in a wet cubicle, white tiles smeared with something brown-red like dried blood. Nobody was around him, so he pushed up the blindfold to his forehead. He said to himself, *Madre de dios, I am now reaping the hatred of the yakuza that I ordered killed, Dios mio, save me from death, and I promise I will never do it again, I will run away from the don and change my life to a better one, for the sake of my small Bonita.* That was his small prayer for a God whom he perceived to be the Almighty Savior.

The cubicle was chest high. If one stood, he would be able to see the view all around, like in the office of Don Victorini. Every time he went there, all the pretty faces would pop out and say, "Hi Sali, I am free tonight for a dinner date." He would just throw them a flying kiss and a wink. Henrietta, his beloved, the mother of his Bonita, was too clean to be smeared with infidelity by him.

He was too afraid to peep out of the cubicle. His whole body ached from fear. He could hear clearly that there were violent movements around, stomping of heavy boots just nearby, maybe behind his cubicle. It made him afraid to turn his face because he might see the face of his tormentor, and he did not want to bring it to his memory, even in his death.

But in the cubicle facing him, he saw the faces of two of his captors. They were not Japanese; they were bearded Arabs. *What the hell is happening?* he asked himself.

Then he heard weak, tired moaning just above. Within his upper visual field, he could see the heads and the shoulders of well-built men, strong and muscular with only their white, dirty, thin vests on. Their muscles were bulging, shiny, and dirty with maybe mud or blood.

A heavily accented man said, "So, he do not know anything then."

Someone answered, "Heez yuuzless. He down't know naathin."

A baritone voice said, "Dazz okay. Get the bag and the machete. The bigger chunks will be for the fishes in the ocean, and the smaller ones will be for the maggots in the forest as it used to be. Is that clear?"

"Yes, Barroodi." Another heavily accented voice.

The man who was screaming was now pleading for his life.

"Please . . . I have a family. I have a son and two daughters. My wife is in the hospital. They are waiting for me."

The baritone voice answered, "I will reverse your situation. From now on, they will no longer wait for you. But you will be the one to wait for them." He paused, and then continued. "You will wait for them in hell," he said, "or maybe heaven."

Salvador saw above him the muscular arms raise the machete and as quick as the wind slashed it down. A crashing and slicing sound with a deafening scream of pain from the pleading man penetrated Salvador's skull with true terror. He could not move even an inch from his fetal position; he was severely shocked by the horror he had just witnessed. The machete was continuously moving up and down, violently splashing blood all over. Several times, warm blood spurted on him. One side of his face, head, and shoulder were already smeared with blood, as if he was the one bleeding. He experienced the never-ending horror of his life. He wished it would end in an instant, but at the same time he did not want it to end, because he knew he would be next.

Suddenly, it stopped. All the scenes were clearly imprinted in his mind, very vivid in his memory.

The baritone voice said, "I will rest for a while. I know that there will be another one waiting for me before the night is over. Make it quick. I want to go home before sunrise."

He heard all the movements, the splashing and swishing sound of the pieces of the flesh being placed inside a bag or two. After all those movements, he heard heavy washing. At this moment, he gained the courage to move his limbs. Slowly he moved. Getting on all fours like a newborn dog, he crawled to a small opening. When he reached the edge, he saw bloody, heavy boots in front of his face. He screamed inside his brain, *O my God. If you are really a God, create a miracle and save from me from this horror.*

As if God had heard him, the heavily accented voice said,

"Ask him now, we are in a hurry. Barroodi wants to go home before sunrise. Remember, the second body should be dumped outside the don's mansion."

Salvador knew they were talking about him. Inside his chest, there was a tightness he had never felt before. *God, don't forsake me now. I promise I will be a good person. Show me your power.*

The bloody man in front of Salvador gave him a paper and pen, and said, "We want to communicate with the assassin of the Yakuza clan." Salvador heard nothing more, but he knew exactly what they wanted.

The heavy accent said, "Write quickly and your life will be spared."

At sunrise, Salvador, still blindfolded, was pushed out of the van. He heard the van speed away, and then it was gone. He removed the blindfold. He was right in front of their house, his home. He saw the faint light in the kitchen where his wife was preparing breakfast. He was expected. He jumped toward his home, heavy tears rolling down his cheeks as if this were the first time he had seen his house after a million years.

Detective Fielder said, "That was easy."

He was holding the paper where Salvador had written down the way to contact Resty. It was just a phone number and the words *dial X4.*

He continued. "But I enjoyed the play." He raised his face to the Arab performers, friends of Jamila, and said, "Guys, you should be in the Van Helsing Booth of the Universal Studios."

Jamila said, "Did you see how pale he was? Don Victorini would never have recognized him. His most trusted man turned into dough."

The performers laughed. The heavily accented man said in simple English, pure California accent, "I thought he gave me the winning Lotto number in Mega Millions."

Everyone laughed.

The next day. In Detective Mark Fielder's office.

"Thank God, I had a wonderful rest yesterday. After we got the assassin's number, I was so relieved," Detective Amin was saying.

"If your ruse didn't work, what would you have done next?" asked Detective Fielder.

"I would have kept you in charge of the torture until we got what we wanted, and promised you that I would not arrest you for police brutality." She grinned naughtily.

Someone was knocking on the door. Detective Fielder said, "Come in, it's open."

"Tom, I'm glad you came." Detective Fielder spread his arms, as did the engineer, and they hugged. Detective Amin shrugged.

They noticed. Releasing each other, Detective Fielder introduced them. "Detective Amin, meet engineer Thomas Brown, my childhood friend. We were neighbors, went to the same grade school, graduated from the same high school, went on to different careers, and met in person after fifteen long years."

"No wonder you miss each other so much." Detective Amin extended her hand to shake Tom's hand.

"Sit down, guys." Mark closed and locked the door. He continued. "In fifteen minutes, I will take you to Hometown Buffet, my treat. But first, let us discuss a very important and delicate matter. No one should know this except for us three. I trust you both with my life and my career."

Tom smiled and said, "Get to the point, my friend. You know me from the start. I don't waste time."

"I am going to call somebody; I don't know how long the conversation will last. Will you be able to locate him?" Mark asked Tom.

"The moment he picks up the phone and says hello, he's already located. Let's go to Hometown Buffet right now if your problem is that simple to make me drive over five hundred miles. I'm literally starving." Tom stood up and walked toward the door. The two followed.

While eating, Tom asked Detective Fielder, "When do you plan to make that call?"

"Tonight," Detective Fielder answered.

"Well and good," Tom said.

Detective Amin asked, "After we have located the subject, how are we going to approach him?"

Detective Fielder looked at Detective Amin and said, "I know that you know the answer to that question, and I agree with it."

"I just don't know which planet you're from," Detective Amin said, raising her knife and fork up to shoulder level and then continuing to eat.

Tom stood up to get a second helping.

Detective Fielder faced Detective Amin and said, "Tom is a rare kind of communications engineer. When we were in grade school, he recorded our teacher's lesson without using a tape recorder or a microphone, just three simple wires and two diodes. I don't know how, but I know why. That's the simplest way I can put it."

Detective Amin said, without looking, "I trust you of course. And I don't distrust him, you know."

"I know, but you don't look very confident in him," said Detective Fielder.

"Aren't we all? Detectives are suspicious by nature, you know that," she said.

Tom arrived and said to Detective Amin, "Don't believe everything he says, he can always flatter you."

He put down his plate and a small gadget, pressed the small

button, and they listened to their previous conversation while Tom was away.

Detective Amin said, not lifting her face from the food, "I told you so. We cannot have privacy around this engineer."

The trio laughed.

They stopped at Circuit City; Tom purchased some tiny copper wires, connectors, and plugs for his computer. Then they went to Detective Mark Fielder's house.

Tom busied himself constructing a mini-communications center on the center table of Detective Fielder's house, using his own laptop computer with a strange kind of software that he programmed himself, while watching the Discovery Channel.

Detective Amin faced Detective Fielder and broke the silence. "Is it possible that our subject also has a way of tracing our call to your house?"

"That's exactly what's on my mind. That's why I don't want to do this anywhere except my house with me as the bait," Detective Fielder said, bright-eyed.

Tom finished, and explained. "This is the detailed map of the world. Wherever the caller is, the computer screen will automatically focus on the locality of the caller." He pointed to his computer screen, then he pointed, and ran his finger over the wires he had meticulously connected to the phone wire and said, "And this is the trap. My program will automatically locate the phone the moment he picks it up. And presto, there he is, and here you are, time for you to do your things."

Detective Amin made a few phone calls, mostly coordinating with their assigned SWAT team in that area. She alerted everyone to be on the lookout for a dangerous and armed criminal.

At 10 p.m., when there was less traffic and fewer people, Detective Fielder was in front of the phone, hands perspiring, and excited.

He picked it up in his left hand, pressed it against his ear, placed it back in its cradle, and said, "There was a dial tone."

"We know there was a dial tone!" Detective Amin almost shouted, very nervous, too.

"What am I going to say? Pose as a client trying to hire him? To kill someone? Offer money? Ask for his price? What?" Detective Fielder asked.

Tom lifted his eyes from the Discovery Channel and said, "No, my friend! You introduce yourself, because the moment you call him, he already knows who you are. Tell him you are coming to arrest him for such and such a crime. And boom, he'll panic."

"I pray it is that easy. First, I don't have an arrest warrant," Detective Fielder said and continued, "second, he has not been identified."

Detective Amin said, "Just tell him he is wanted for questioning. Read him the Miranda warning if you want, even if he is not under arrest. You're just nervous."

"No! I'm not. You're making fun of me," Detective Fielder shouted, releasing his own tension.

He picked up the phone. He did not put it to his ear. He placed it back on its cradle. He pressed the button for speaker mode. He dialed the number. The first was a single ring and then an electronic voice message: *The number you dialed is not yet in service.* He dialed a second time. Another electronic message: *We're sorry, the number is not complete as dialed, please check the number and dial again.* He dialed a third time. There was a long dial tone, and then it went dead. The fourth time he dialed, the phone rang.

On the third ring, it was picked up, and a voice said, "Do you need my services?" It was a penetrating voice, sweet and chilly, not short of terrifying.

Tom raised his hand, catching the attention of Detective Amin,

71

and pointed to his computer screen, which showed the location of the caller. Detective Amin went ahead and dialed the SWAT Hotline.

"This is Detective Mark Fielder."

"I know. I have caller ID. Do you need my services?"

"No. I am coming to arrest you."

They heard a crisp laugh. The most terrifying laugh they had ever heard in their lives. And the line stayed on; it did not go dead as expected. The voice faded away and then one second of silence.

Detective Amin had just finished her call to the SWAT team, which she did the moment the light blinked at the corner of Harvard and Third Street. The area was already being surrounded by the SWAT teams who started coming with other teams.

Tom's ears were wide open, still listening. They heard stealthy footsteps, a lot of them. Then they heard a faint voice, like a whisper. "In that corner."

Tom said, "He left the phone hanging and ran for cover. He's in the bag, if your SWAT team is as good as you said."

They heard again, "Sir, nobody is in here."

Detective Fielder was in communication with the team and said, "Hey, guys, this is Detective Mark Fielder. Do not touch anything in there. Do not touch the phone. It is already a crime scene. Keep it as untouched as possible. I'm coming."

They heard an answer. "Detective Fielder, this is Sergeant Mendoza. There is no telephone here; you're on a transistor radio."

They heard some background comments. "Is this a radio program of a sort? I prefer television."

Detective Fielder stood up and signaled to Detective Amin, who had just put down the phone. She called a team from Crime Scene Investigation, to collect anything of value to identify everyone who had entered that room, with a request to save the transistor radio. He had something special for it.

"Tom, make yourself at home. I'll be back in an hour or two," Detective Fielder said, pointing a finger at his friend on their way out.

When they reached the deserted, unfinished house, Detective Amin put the radio inside a plastic bag. They were going to bring it to Dr. Yokohama at the LAPD crime lab, as the first true subject for the doctor.

Five-thirty in the afternoon, three days later.
Dr. Yokohama was on the phone urging the detectives to come immediately.

In the doctor's laboratory, he showed the detectives the recordings. "Your subject has been on the move in big circles all day long, but for the past thirty minutes, he was just in a small circle. This is his house."

"How did you do that?" Detective Fielder asked.

"Inside the panel I scraped something unusual, it could be dried sweat, or a teardrop, or saliva, for DNA. That radio was modified to serve another purpose," Doctor Yokohama said.

Detective Amin went again to the phone, alerted the SWAT team, again to arrest a dangerous armed criminal. She gave the address.

Thirty minutes later...
They went to police headquarters. Whether the subject was invited or arrested, it didn't matter now. What mattered was their assignment was over.

They met the suspect in the interrogation room: a big-bellied, elderly, balding guy, not short of obese, wearing double-thick eyeglasses and a severely old, worn, checkered shirt and jeans.

Detective Fielder did his best in a grueling interrogation, like a very hungry lion in sheep's clothing.

Detective Amin's conclusion on their case, based on the suspect's interview, was that it was far from over. The suspect, Michael Jones, said, "I repair hundreds of radios, besides my subcontracted work from Radio Shack, Best Buy, Wal-Mart, and Circuit City, anytime their customers return it to them. I won't be able to remember them all."

Michael Jones's own life story lingered in his memory, one which he would take to the grave without telling anyone.

A year ago, he had made that dreadful phone call.

"I am just a poor man, compared to what you are or what you have. I have no means to get what I want, but I am willing to pay you with all my life's savings, just to get the man who killed my daughter," Michael Jones was in tears.

"And how much is that?" the man he called had asked.

Mr. Jones answered, "Twenty-one thousand four hundred eighty-two dollars and eighty-six cents."

"And who is the man you want killed?" Mr. Jones was asked.

He answered, "The man who raped and killed my nine-year-old daughter."

"Name and address?"

Mr. Jones explained, "It has already been eighteen months, and the police still don't have a clue, just smears of his secretions, which I hate to hear."

Mr. Jones heard the scolding voice: "You don't have enough money. You don't have any identity. Don't you think it's a double job for me?"

"I agree. But I don't have anything more to offer."

"What do you do for a living?"

"I am a radio-TV technician; I also repair electronic home appliances, microwaves, coffee makers, electric fans, many things."

"That job doesn't pay much, does it?"

"No. It does not."

"You lost your daughter," the voice trailed a sound, and then asked, "how much is a life worth, if you may calculate its cost?"

"Millions of dollars cannot pay it," he answered angrily.

"Then you are actually not paying me anything, to take a life of another person, don't you think?" the person on the other line asked.

"Ye . . . ye . . . yes, but I have nothing more than my own life," Mr. Jones said.

"I cannot take your life as a payment, but why don't you offer me your services, like repairing my home appliances for life."

Relieved, Mr. Jones answered, "Yes! Yes! I am very willing to do that, just to get that bastard."

"Then it's a deal."

"Yes."

The person asked, "How many days from now do you want this person killed?"

"I will not constrain you with a schedule, but I would be very happy if it is very soon, or at least while I'm still alive."

"Sorry, I work on a schedule; I have other jobs to do. Let's say four days?"

"Very well, then," Mr. Jones answered.

"My deal is I get paid half today, and the rest will be after the job is done. You give me the amount you mentioned, and the other half, which is your services, I'll collect after the job is done, is that clear?"

"Yes."

"Now, go to Griffith Park, walk up the hill, put down your money on the third bench that you find, and I'll come and collect it. The other half, which is your services to me, I'll collect after the job is done. Is that clear?"

"Yes."

Day One. Resty started to work. Starting with the scene of the crime. The rapist killer did not use force to enter the house. So it was someone who had access to the house or somebody known to the household members, or at least familiar.

He made a list of all the people who had access to the house, then a list of all the family acquaintances, then a list of all the people who could just knock at the door and be let in normally. The list went on and on.

Now was the time to eliminate those on the list one by one.

The list was reduced to four subjects: the milkman, the FedEx deliveryman, the plumber, and the group of people who went from house to house distributing religious reading materials.

Cancel the milkman because he comes only in the morning. The crime happened between two in the afternoon and five. The FedEx deliveryman might have seen something and not remember it, but he works within a schedule. He cannot waste time raping and killing a child. If it was the plumber, then that wouldn't have been missed by skillful detectives; there would be traces of plumbing work all over, his DNA test came out negative.

It was time to listen to religious sermons then.

Day Two. Resty, dressed in semi-formal wear, and went inside the temporary makeshift church. He sat beside an elderly lady.

Resty leaned near the lady and said, "I am not a member, but I am searching."

"A lost sheep is always welcome to the house of God," the lady answered.

The pastor was giving a tearful sermon. "Jesus is behind us, we shall not be moved. Just like a strong bridge, standing over raging flood water, year after year."

Rusty leaned again against the shoulder of the lady and said, "How do I get baptized in your church?"

The lady was startled by what she heard, and exclaimed, "I'll introduce you to the pastor right away."

The lady was one of the biggest donors of the church. After the sermon, the pastor approached and thanked the lady for her presence. The lady said, "Pastor, we found another lost sheep. This young man here wants to be among your flock. He wishes to be baptized immediately."

After the shedding of tears of joy from the members over Resty's baptism, the work began again.

Resty said, "Pastor, I want to travel on your path. I wish to be with you wherever you go to gather lost sheep."

The pastor said, "My child, the work of my church is to go out and look for lost sheep. Everyone goes in pairs; I will assign you to be with Sister Mildred."

"How about you, dear pastor? Whom do you go out with?" asked Resty.

"I go out only with Jesus," answered the pastor.

Day Three, 4 p.m. The pastor was brought to the Emergency Room.

5 p.m. Mr. Jones arrived home, shocked by the thing he found on his table, and called 911.

In the police crime laboratory, it was confirmed by DNA that the penis on the plate of Mr. Jones's table belonged to the one who had molested and killed his daughter.

Day Four. The pastor died a slow and painful death. Nothing could stop the bleeding from his severed penis. He received a total of twenty blood transfusions to no avail.

Mr. Jones was at home, sitting on the sofa, still in shock. The phone rang, and Mr. Jones answered it. "Hello?"

"I am ready to collect the other half of your payment, Mr. Jones."

"You have my lifetime services. Call me anytime, twenty-four seven, I am available for you."

It was just a year-old memory. At present, he would get phone calls with instructions on modifying transistor radios and leaving them in some weird place at weird times of the day or night.

He was released and went his way, after an extensive interrogation by the detectives who suspected his connection to what they thought was vigilante work, but there was no strong evidence or motive to connect him.

Mr. Jones went back to his normal life. He was self-employed, and he had regular customers.

Several months after the pastor died of severe hemorrhage, Mr. Jones went on with his life, of working here and there, and he was able to gain his life back. He started making friends again, sitting and joking with younger people whenever he was called into business offices repairing coffeemakers, microwaves, fax machines, photocopiers, and other stuff.

He had known the late Mr. Oliver Stonel and his widow, Mrs. Margaret Stonel, since he was single. They were two of his oldest clients, the owners of ten cargo planes, who had had a franchised FedEx delivery service for almost fifteen years now. Once in a while, Mr. Jones also served as their handyman. Today, he was in their office fixing the coffeemaker.

"It's only three, why are you here?" Mrs. Margaret Stonel asked her daughter, who had come home from school early. They usually went home together at five, Monday to Friday. She dropped her daughter at eight at the school gate, and at four-thirty she walked two blocks from school to the office.

"Shortened period. I think the school's having some sort of a meeting," Elizabeth said. She was sixteen years old, a vibrant and happy-go-lucky teenager.

"You're not sure? You don't know what's going on in your school?" Mrs. Stonel said.

"Mom, when Miss Rodriguez was making the announcement,

I was talking to Clarice," Elizabeth answered.

"You're not paying attention then," Mrs. Stonel said, stood up and walked toward Mr. Jones, the repairman.

"Oh Mom, it's all the same. What matters is I'm out of school early. Do you have anything to eat here?"

"No."

"I'm hungry. I want to eat something."

"What do you want?'

"Some chips, of course, Pringles or Lays, something like that."

"Ralph's is just across the street. Buy anything you want. Honey, would you mind buying something for the girls? Mr. Jones is almost done with the coffeemaker."

Mrs. Margaret Stonel ran the business with enough profit every year that allowed them to live a comfortable life. The office was composed mostly of young ladies, new graduates, working as office clerks, Mario the office boy, and the delivery personnel outside most of the time. Mrs. Stonel treated everyone as her family, which was why her business ran smoothly.

It was already four-fifteen, and Elizabeth was not back yet.

"It's fifteen minutes past our coffee break," one of the girls commented.

"I'm starting to worry now," Mrs. Stonel said, rubbing both palms together to warm them up. Her hands were getting colder.

Even Mario's not back yet. I sent him to follow her at four, to help her carry the stuff."

Mario arrived and said, "Ma'am, I went all over Ralph's and the other stores around. I did not find her."

"Coffee is ready, the coffeemaker works well," Mr. Jones said jokingly.

The phone rang.

Mrs. Stonel picked it up and said, "Hello?"

She heard Elizabeth, who sounded very frightened and crying, with words between sobs, said, "Mom, it's dark in here, please get me, I'm scared . . ."

Mrs. Stonel heard her sudden scream and a loud crashing braaannngggg. She stood up, and then the line went dead. She was shocked, unable to move, turned very pale and missed the chair, fell to the floor, awake, mouth open, lips trembling and weakly talking.

Mr. Jones was frightened. The girls quickly attended to her.

"Ma'am, what happened? What was that?"

She felt very weak, and her vision was blurred. "It was Elizabeth. I think she's been abducted."

"Oh my God," one of the girls shouted, and panic started in the office.

"Let's call the police."

At four-thirty, one of the girls came and said, "Ma'am, the police said that they need twenty-four hours before a person can be reported missing."

"By that time my daughter could be dead."

Mr. Jones's heart sunk. He remembered his dead daughter. He had worked with the late Mr. Stonel for twenty years. He was their only repairman, at home and in the office. He had known Mrs. Stonel for a long time. He had seen her when she was pregnant. He had seen and played with Elizabeth since she was a small girl. He could not let this happen.

"I know of somebody who can help us," Mr. Jones said.

Everybody looked at him. They knew him well. They knew what had happened to his daughter, raped and killed. The killer was also found in a very mysterious way, and bled to death.

"I actually don't know him. It is just a phone number and a deal."

"Just make that deal. Call him immediately, please. I want my daughter unharmed. Oh my God." Mrs. Stonel was sobbing, and pressing her hands against her face.

"Mrs. Stonel, you have to make that phone call and make the deal yourself."

"How can I do that?"

"Please be strong for Elizabeth. You cannot be weak now, especially at this moment. Please make the call before it's too late."

Everyone understood what he meant.

At four thirty-five, she made the call. The first was a single ring and then an electronic voice message: *The number you dialed is not a working number.*

"That's not a working number!" Mrs. Stonel screamed in panic.

Mr. Jones said, "Dial again. It's really like that; I think he's trying to trace the call. Please keep on dialing until you get an answer."

She dialed a second time. Another electronic message: *We're sorry, the number is not complete as dialed, please check the number and dial again.* She dialed a third time. There was a long dial tone, and then it went dead. The fourth time she dialed, the phone rang.

"Do you need my services?" A deep and cold voice.

She hesitated at first, and then nervously answered, "Yeesss! I think my daughter has been abducted. I need her returned unharmed."

"Why call me?" the phone went dead.

Everybody was in shock, panic around.

"Please dial again, Mrs. Stonel. Plead with him. Offer him money or anything."

She dialed again.

"It is you again."

She screamed, "Please don't hang up. The life of my daughter is in your hands now."

"Tell me what you want and be quick."

"I'm going to give you a million dollars, maybe more, just get my daughter alive."

"My services are to get someone killed, not to get someone alive."

"I'll double your price, just get her."

"You don't know my price."

"Mr. Jones will tell me."

"Put him on the phone."

Mrs. Stonel handed the phone to Mr. Jones and said, "He wants to speak with you."

Mr. Jones was frightened but took the phone. "Hello?"

"Mr. Jones, I'm happy with your work for me. But I am not happy now." Mr. Jones trembled.

Mr. Jones gathered his wits and said, "Please. Elizabeth's life could be hanging by a thread now. She left the office after three. Her mother received a phone call between four-fifteen and four-thirty I suppose. Mrs. Stonel collapsed, and she said she's been abducted."

"Let everybody go home. Enjoy their dinner. I'll call Mrs. Margaret Stonel tonight for my professional fee."

Five minutes after five, the work began. Robert Flang, the chief of the Accounts and Billing Department, was just getting inside his car to go home after office hours, when he felt a sudden sharp stabbing pain behind his left knee. Reflexively, he grabbed it and saw the blood spurting vigorously. He almost fainted, but somebody tied a thick rubber band just above the knee.

A very strange voice told him, "Don't look behind. If you don't get to the hospital in an hour, you're dead. If you get to the hospital after forty-five minutes, you lose your leg. If you don't do as I tell you, you die now. Quickly make a choice."

"What do you want?" Robert Flang answered.

"Give me the address of the one who called this number between four-fifteen and four-thirty," the stranger told him and handed him the number of the office of Mrs. Stonel, where Elizabeth made that mysterious phone call.

"It could be several."

"Then give them all to me."

Under Robert Flang were several units; one of them was the phone company's backbone, the billing system. They billed both the caller and the receiver of the call. He could trace anyone who used a phone. He limped, holding both ends of the rubber band, keeping it tight, saving his own blood as much as possible. He could feel the sharp instrument behind him. He knew that this guy was serious, and he was ready to do a nephrectomy right then and there.

There were only two calls between those times. First at ten past four from the pizza delivery place, and the second was at four-sixteen from 325 Sixth Street.

Robert Flang handed the two billing addresses behind him, and dialed 911. The guy took the paper and left.

Elizabeth was on the damp floor of a dark basement, half conscious, dried blood all over her face, severely beaten. Resty picked her up and carried her to the back of the tinted-window Lincoln Navigator. He drove to Mrs. Stonel's residence and called.

Twelve past six in the evening, Mrs. Stonel was crying in front of the TV, scared to death that something bad might have happened to her only child. Then the phone rang.

"Hello?"

The voice said, "Mrs. Stonel. Please hang up and dial nine-one-one, get the paramedics, she needs to be in the hospital immediately. She's at your front door."

She panicked, ran to the door and found the unconscious

Elizabeth, face swollen and covered in blood. She went to the phone and called 911. In less than six minutes, the paramedics came and took her to the hospital.

The police investigators, at this early stage, did not find a clue.

Early the next morning, in a dark alley way behind the Ralph's near Mrs. Stonel's office, there was a large gathering of onlookers. Sirens came from different directions. A man was hanging on a pole upside down with all his intestines hanging down to the ground, the blood and dirt covered with flies. He was the sole resident of 325 Sixth Street.

After a week, Elizabeth was half recovered. She could eat on her own and could walk with a walker. Detective Fielder and Detective Amin introduced themselves and showed her the picture of Daniel Arce, the resident of 325 Sixth Street.

Elizabeth trembled in fear, fell on her bed, and cried, "Take it away from me."

"He cannot harm you now. He's dead," Detective Fielder said.

Elizabeth stopped trembling. She felt suddenly safe.

"Now tell us what happened."

"I took the shorter way to Ralph's, the alleyway behind. Then somebody from behind suddenly grabbed my arms. When I looked, it was that man. It was very quick. I saw his knuckles coming to my face. The next thing I remember is that I was fighting and being touched all over my body and being beaten on the face and thighs at the same time. Then I think I lost consciousness again. When I woke up, I think I was in a basement or something. When I adjusted my eyes, I saw a phone. I called the office. I heard my mother's voice. I cried. The door suddenly opened, and he hit the phone with something, maybe a baseball bat. Then I felt a blow on my face, repeatedly, and then I felt nothing more.

"Then the next thing I remember . . . I heard a soft voice, like an angel. I couldn't open my eyes. The voice told me, I was sent by your mother to get you. Then the voice asked me, where did that guy pick you up? Then I remember I answered, behind the Ralph's alleyway. Then I think I passed out again.

"Then I remember voices, people on the rush and saying something like gauze and scissors. Then nothing. Next thing I remember was the face of my mother, crying in front of my face, and I asked her, what happened? And she told me, 'You're safe now, my darling, what happened does not matter anymore.'"

"Mrs. Stonel, based on your previous statement, don't you think Mr. Jones is connected to this?"

"The only connection I see with Mr. Jones was . . . he offered a way to get my daughter back alive."

"You said that you offered a one-million-dollar reward for the safe return of your daughter."

"Yes, but it was never collected."

The detectives left the hospital.

Detective Fielder said, "Another dead end, and the same pattern."

"No. I think another link," Detective Amin said. "Our assassin is also a vigilante."

"Aren't you surprised how he located his target?" Detective Fielder asked.

"I think . . . no, I'm sure he has a criminal mind, and he can put his shoes exactly where the criminal was. That's why he can guess where he could find his target," Detective Amin concluded.

"So far, not all his targets are criminals. Just anybody whose death has been paid for," Detective Fielder said.

Chapter 6
The Proposal

Detective Mark Fielder explained to Captain Montero, "With all due respect, sir, our assignment is not as easy as I thought it was." He continued, "We need a team, mainly Detective Amin and me, also Thomas and Doctor Yokohama, and give me some of your experts on detection and surveillance."

"I'll try to pull some strings, maybe borrow a hand or two from Homeland Security and from my friends in the FBI. I'll give you a call as soon as I get the approval. Don't forget, it's the taxpayers' money you are spending here. Don't let this hunt be very expensive," Captain Montero said.

After three days, Detective Fielder received a phone call from Captain Montero. "Gather your friends; your team will be on the payroll starting tomorrow at exactly eight in the morning."

"Thank you so very much, sir." He called Detective Amin with the news.

The group was composed of eight especially hand picked for this job.

Their code name: Taskforce Predator.

Three persons were responsible for the communications part.

A young, gorgeous lady, Betti Crungle, could identify almost any kind of sound, voice, or musical note. When she was twelve, she participated in a local "Name That Tune" competition, and in the maximum of three notes she was able to name the song. She could identify different kinds of birds just by listening to their sounds. She could identify any radio announcer. Once she heard a voice, she would never forget it, and she could differentiate it from any other voice, whether it was on the phone, on the radio, or in person.

Josh Aaron was a young punk, communications wizard, who would collaborate with Thomas Brown. Their assignment was to locate where the speaker was coming from. Both could quickly make out coordinates and triangulate where the origin was. Josh could locate anyone on a cell phone in less than five seconds.

The third was a computer guy, Crete Belder, a notorious hacker, now an adopted son of the FBI. He created his own software unknown to any computer master. English was just his second language; electronic language was his first. He could hack into any computer wherever it was. He could actually communicate with any computer; ask a computer who's its registered owner, its user, its location as if he was talking to a friend.

Dr. Yokohama teamed up with Shilin Ming, an electronics engineer originally from Taiwan. She knew all the parts of any electronic equipment. If you dismantled five different electronic appliances and mixed them together, Shilin would assemble the five different appliances in less than an hour.

The next morning, the super eight had a breakfast meeting at a lounge at the Marriot Hotel. Mostly, they told personal stories and jokes. Getting to know each other was the main point of the meeting. The real meeting would be in one of the LAPD safe houses. It would be used as the headquarters for the team. All the equipment they required would be available when they arrived there.

Everyone was excited when they arrived at the safe house. It was like a little mansion, arranged like a puzzle, where one might open a restroom door while intending to go out of the house. Nina, a blonde in office attire, oriented them to the place. The basement will be their lair, an exceptionally large area, a fully equipped surveillance laboratory, with five sides; each one had a large monitor screen, and each monitor could be divided into forty-eight different tiny monitors.

At the center was their worktable. They set up a trap. Detective Fielder would make the call; it would be recorded for voice analysis, would be stored in their gigantic voice database, to find if they had a match. The phone that he would use was his home phone, to make it appear that he was at home making the phone call.

Each one made himself busy constructing the trap; everyone was desperate to locate their subject, code name "Paid Killer."

For the youngsters, this was a sort of competition of who got it first, a very personal matter for them; but for the elders, this was just another job, nothing personal.

Betti was fixing the wires of her digital super audio recorder. She soldered the ends of its wires to the audio receiver wires of the telephone that they were going to use to call Resty. She insulated each line of wire using a glue gun. She connected the USB wire of the recorder to the USB port of her laptop and tested the signal of the sound waves. Green and blue lines appeared on the screen, and she raised her arms with a triumphant smile.

Josh and Thomas were busy connecting the wires to the diodes that they fixed on the U.S. map, the map of California and the map of L.A. on the wall.

Josh looked at Thomas and said, "Tom, I'll go up for a while and fix these things on the roof top."

Thomas said, "Do you need a hand?"

"Nope. I'm okay."

Josh went out carrying three boxes and two plastic bags and went to the roof top. The sun was still cold and just coming into view above the mountain along the horizon. He pulled out the hammer gun and mimicked a police officer and said playfully, "Freeze or I'll blow your brains out," shrugged his shoulder and went back to work. He mounted three dish antennas on the roof top to pick up cell site signals; he positioned the satellite signal finder and tracking meter, which he connected to a descrambler. He looked at the clouds, checking for any signs of rain coming. Satisfied that there was none from the clear blue sky, went to the edge of the roof and let loose the wires until they reached the windows where he will get them from inside to connect to the telephone lines and then to Crete's computer.

Shilin Ming and Dr. Yokohama were sitting near the window coffee table and on it was the confiscated radio and several of their tiny electronic tools.

Pointing to the red wire with his thin Philip screw driver, Dr. Yokohama asked, "Why do you think this useless wire is connected between the speaker and the RF?"

"That is not useless. It will actually alter the frequency of the speaker." Shilin said.

"We are here just as a backup support. You are here in case they need a hand if anything malfunctions. But me, I am here in case they pick up something for me to locate." Dr. Yokohama was smiling.

Crete Belder was in front of his 21-inch laptop. He stretched his neck, waved and called out to Detective Amin. "I'm logged in to the local telephone company and three cell site companies. What's next?"

Detective Amin said, "The waiting game."

The whole day was busy for everyone, putting together what they needed, or contacting their personal contacts when some delicate part was not available, until nightfall. They went out for a late dinner. They were a bit quiet now, trying to ease their minds and bodies from the day's work and imagining the next day's event, when Detective Mark Fielder would actually call the "Paid Killer."

When they went back to the safe house, each one was alone in his room. Not one of them had a good night's sleep; their minds were still very active, imagining what was to come.

The next morning after breakfast, everything was set. At ten in the morning, everyone was sitting around their workstations, excited.

Detective Fielder was very nervous again this time. In front of him was an on button that, when pushed, was just like picking up a phone ready to dial a number.

He pushed the button and dialed the number of the "Paid Killer."

There was a single ring and then an electronic voice message: *The number you dialed is not a working number.* He dialed a second time. Another electronic message: *We're sorry, the number is not complete as dialed, please check the number and dial again.* He dialed a third time, there was a long dial tone, and then it went dead. The fourth time he dialed, the phone rang.

Someone picked up and said, "To thee I wisheth bright mornin'. Detective Mark Fielder, I know thou don't need my services. As I told thou before, I have caller ID. I also happen to know thee are not in thy house, and I know thou are not coming to arrest me."

"You are correct in one thing, but most of it is wrong."

"At least I did not get zero, unlike most of you who will get

91

zero today."

Josh signaled to everyone pointing to the wall L.A. map. There were four blinking lights, one in Pasadena, one in Venice Beach, one in Downtown L.A., corner of Broadway and Ord, and the fourth one was their safe house.

"I need your services."

"Who do you want to die?"

"How much would you charge to kill one person?"

"It depends on who you want to die and when."

"How much would you charge me, if I want you to kill yourself?"

"Oh! Not an easy target. First I don't know where to locate me, second I don't know if I would be able to kill me."

Crete printed the detailed maps of the whereabouts of the blinking lights. He stood up, picked up the printed materials and went to Detective Amin. Crete put his finger across his lips indicating to keep quiet. Detective Amin looked at it and went to the next room to make a phone call to local police headquarters in those areas.

"It's very easy, just jump out of your window."

"It does not guarantee death if the target lives in a bungalow."

"Then kill yourself in the most fitting manner that you wish, like the body found behind the Ralph's alleyway."

"How can a hurricane destroy itself? How can an earthquake crush itself or a lightning burn itself? When two hurricanes meet, they will not destroy each other; they will join forces and destroy whatever is in their path with combined strength."

"I can see you are a very intelligent person, Mister Paid Killer."

"You can call me Resty, that's what everyone calls me."

"I can see you are a very intelligent person, Mister Resty."

"Goodbye for now." The phone went dead, and a plain dial

tone sounded.

"We got him this time!" Tom and Josh shouted in unison.

Detective Fielder looked at Betti and Detective Amin, and asked them, "How about you two, were you able to ID his voice?"

Betti answered, "Yes."

"And who is he?"

"Chucky."

"Whaaat?"

"Remember *Child's Play*? Chucky the Good Guy thing turned killer, Charles Lee Ray."

"Charles Lee Ray was a fictional character; could you please speak English?"

"What I mean was, there were thousands and thousands with exactly the same voice and sound as the one you have just called. It was an electronic voice, not human."

Everyone was perplexed.

"But I can find him," Josh interjected.

"What you will find is just an abandoned transistor radio in an abandoned building."

"I can talk to that machine," Crete Belder said. Everyone looked at him, in his quiet and dark corner.

"Would you be able to really do that?"

"Of course."

"But you don't have our subject on line."

"But I will know how and where the machine is."

"Let's try that one then. Talk to the machine."

The local police force was able to locate the building where the signal was coming from. It was from the New Science Building opposite Fuller Theological Seminary in North Los Robles in Pasadena. In a matter of minutes, the building was surrounded with sharpshooters. The SWAT team scanned the surroundings for possible booby traps. Everything was clear. The K-9 team was excited to follow the lead. Five trained German shepherds entered with the team, but did not find any living being anywhere. After the search, as instructed by the LAPD, they cordoned the area with the usual yellow, do-not-cross police line barriers, for the CSI. The team was able to retrieve a transistor radio from the roof top.

The second blinking light was from Venice Beach. Josh and Tom were able to triangulate the exact location. It was at the end part of the Pier. Detective Fielder and Detective Amin were able to find an abandoned, low-battery cell phone near the edge, almost ready to fall. Detective Amin picked it up with a gloved hand and placed it inside the plastic evidence container.

The team of LAPD was able to locate an Internet Café on the corner of Main Street and Seventh Street. Sgt. Craig went to the manager and showed his I.D. and told him what was happening. They took the identification, address and telephone number of everyone, and instructed them not to leave town without first calling Sgt. Craig of the Detective Division. Crete, Josh and Tom went inside after all the people were outside.

The manager was very anxious, went to Sgt. Craig and said, "Did I break the law?"

Crete answered, "We can't tell until I personally check one of your computers here."

"Inspect anything you want, sir. I've nothing to hide."

Crete sat down in one of the terminals, logged in and went to the programs. After a few minutes, he said, "I found it. It's an interactive program, downloaded to this computer network." He looked at the manager and asked him, "You never close your computers here, right?"

The manager answered, "Right. We are open twenty-four/seven."

"That's it." Crete took a USB flash drive out from his pocket and copied the program. "I have to take this program to my lab. I have to know what I need to find out."

Chapter 7
Back at the Safe House

The team was carefully dismantling every part of the transistor radio found in Pasadena and the cell phone found in Venice Beach. Shilin was able to locate five different things that were not parts of those electronic items.

"This part does not belong to this transistor radio," Shilin said, holding a tiny transistor. "This one should be a short-wave radio transistor receiver, but it becomes a long wave because it is amplified by the connecting diode to the AM, then goes to the FM band to ignore static sound. That was why it was clear, like you were actually talking to him directly."

"Then we could find out where that small thing came from," Detective Amin said.

"This thing is a basic part; you can buy it anywhere or disconnect it from any old or new radio transistor. And even if your radio does not have it, your radio transistor will still function normally," Shilin said. "The same little transistor appeared in the cell phone."

"So, the same part was being used by the Paid Killer wherever he is."

"No. Because the third one is just a program on the PC and the server. It can receive and transmit communication to the domain of the server, but that frequency is unknown to us."

"There is the clue, *that frequency is unknown to us*. We should find that frequency."

"Among the millions and millions, it could take forever. We don't even know if he's using a radio frequency at all."

"We're back to square one then. Doctor Yokohama will try to ID any scrap from those things; sweat, skin, hair, any foreign object that doesn't belong there, including dust and strands of fabric in the dust," Detective Mark Fielder concluded.

Inside the safe house, on the third day, in the basement, the phone rang. Everyone turned and looked at the monitor on top of the worktable; that was supposed to be the phone monitoring the Paid Killer. It was not a real phone; it was a dummy phone, unregistered and no one knew if it had a number. The caller ID said, "Resty to Mark."

Detective Fielder walked toward the phone and sat down while it continued to ring. Everyone walked toward a gadget, to listen and to record everything. No one dared make a sound.

Detective Fielder pushed the button as if he had picked up a regular phone.

"Detective Fielder speaking."

"I know, and I also know a lot more are listening. But I will talk only to you."

"What do you want?"

"I should ask, what do you want?"

"I just want to get you."

"Ah, to get done with it. And after that you'll have another assignment. You'll never get done with it, you know. Your work will never be finished; you will be finished but not the work."

"What's your point?"

96

"I appreciate that you do your work well; I also do my work well. There is nothing personal between us and our work. You go your way, and I'll go my way."

"And if we meet?"

"It could be the beginning of a beautiful friendship."

"It could never be."

"Why?"

"Because I work for the law, and you work against the law."

"You're wrong, Detective Mark Fielder. Both of us work for money, the only difference is I am paid better."

"My work is honorable; yours is dishonorable."

"Wrong again. Remove the money factor; will you work without pay?"

"It doesn't matter now. Sooner or later, you'll fall into our hands, and you'll pay for your crimes."

"Wrong again. I can fall upon you anytime I want, and my crime is already paid. The death of one person can be paid but once." There was laughter, and the line went dead.

"Shakespeare in the voice of R2-D2," Betti said. "This is going nowhere. Paid Killer is using the voices of electronic characters."

"How can he do that?" asked Detective Fielder.

Crete Belder said, "That's easy. Type in the words that you want to say, feed it into the voice mode of the electronic device, and presto. It will say whatever you have typed."

"Wait!" Shilin said brightly, holding the dismantled cell phone. "I almost overlooked the multiple function of this one. In this micro-transistor, I can see an interface, an interactive one— this one—if connected to the SIM card," Shilin was talking while soldering together the pieces she wanted to connect. "Now, try saying this. 'I can see you are a very intelligent person, Mister Paid Killer,'" handing over the microphone to Detective Fielder.

Detective Fielder said, "I can see you are a very intelligent person, Mister Paid Killer."

A voice answered, "You can call me Resty; that's what everyone calls me."

Shilin took the microphone and handed it over to Detective Amin and told her to ask the same thing.

Detective Amin did, and nothing happened. It would not interact with anyone except Detective Fielder.

"Now, let us try this one." Taking the microphone again and giving it to Detective Fielder, Shilin said, "Say this, 'I can see you are a very intelligent person, Mister Resty.'"

Detective Fielder said, "I can see you are a very intelligent person, Mister Resty."

"Goodbye for now." The cell phone went dead.

"He is not only one step ahead of us. He is miles and miles ahead," Josh said.

"What do you mean?" Detective Fielder asked.

Shilin answered, "What he already has is still under experiment in many communications laboratories. It is actually just a theory."

Engineer Tom said, "What she meant was, our subject will talk to us through electronic equipment, without him being actually there, but he can monitor the communications between us and the electronic equipment. He is just listening from somewhere on Earth while you talk to the computer adaptive device."

Josh Aaron leaned forward and said in a low tone, "He can actually be listening to us right now, because he already has the coordinates. He can turn all these electronic devices here into a listening device."

"Can he actually do that?" asked Detective Fielder.

"You're the detective. Find out," Tom said.

Detective Fielder pushed the button and dialed the number.

Out of town. Call again next week. Do not leave a message. It was an answering machine.

Detective Fielder stood up. "He is going for a kill again. Watch the news."

Five days ago, Resty had received a call from London.

"You again, Madam Saeedah. How can I be of service to you this time?"

"You have served me well. It will not be a car crash this time. I want it to be as natural as possible. He's old and sick. I don't want him to outlive this very important meeting. My husband should be in that chair before that meeting."

"Well then."

"I am paying you three times your price six years ago. And it is in full. My assistant will be waiting for your instructions when you call back."

The task force was monitoring world news. Late at night, Detective Amin called Detective Fielder.

"Are you watching CNN?"

"I'm trying to get some sleep, do you mind?"

"Breaking news in Syria; look at it."

The newscaster was saying, *The unpopular second son will be the successor, because the first son is not available. He was involved in a high-speed car crash six years ago and died on the spot. Although the president was old and sick, most of the neighboring leaders were surprised at his sudden death . . .*

"I knew it." Detective Fielder punched the pillow, sat on the edge of the bed, his feet searching for the slippers that were on the other side of the bed. "I'll call our contact about any large amount of cash withdrawals somewhere."

Detective Amin said, "I already did. It was seven days ago, Pakistan."

The task force was busy constructing and reconstructing other

99

gadgets to better understand their prey, so they could lay a better trap.

After two days, the task force laid another trap. They understood that the number of the Paid Killer was not a phone number; it was a radio frequency that could be received and transmitted anywhere, if one knew the frequency.

They put up a frequency meter that gauged the incoming radio frequency, so that they could monitor and listen to that frequency twenty-four hours a day.

The team was again in front of their worktable.

Detective Amin said, "I don't like this."

"Why?" Detective Fielder asked.

Detective Amin stood up. "This is absolute brain work. I want something with legwork. I want something that I can use my eyes in looking for the subject; I want to walk around finding clues. If this does not work, I'm going to go out and start looking. This is not the way I was trained to track down criminals." And she sat down again.

Detective Fielder pushed the button and dialed the number.

"How are you, Detective Fielder? It's you again. Can I be of service to you today?"

"I want to meet you in person," Detective Fielder said.

"Tenth Floor, Suite Ten-two-forty-seven, Ninety-seven-oh-one Wilshire Boulevard, Beverly Hills. In ten minutes." The line went dead.

"Detective Amin, that's your legwork," Detective Fielder said while standing and picking up his jacket and adjusting his government-issued Magnum.

"I better let my fingers do the walking first." She stood up with him and used her cell phone and dialed to activate the SWAT team.

"He knows exactly where we are. Ten minutes' drive from

100

Pacific Eagle Tower," Tom said.

Detective Fielder and Detective Amin went together. Their eyes were quick in scanning all the perimeters when they arrived at the location. They spotted two plainclothes LAPD officers, one young punk in front of the door and a gorgeous tattooed woman in the lobby. They went straight to the elevator and punched the button for the tenth floor. The elevator ascended. Sweat started collecting on Detective Fielder's nose. At last the elevator door opened on the tenth floor. They walked out into the hallway and found the door, 10247. Detective Fielder knocked on the door.

A voice answered, "Come in. It's open."

Detective Fielder touched the door knob; it was as cold as death. He wondered, *What if this was a trap?*

The voice again. "Don't be afraid. Nobody paid me to kill you. I do not kill for free."

Detective Fielder quickly opened the door. Like trained soldiers, the two detectives aimed their handguns at the dark figure in the shadow, comfortably sitting on a swivel chair.

"Please don't bother putting on the lights; they're not working. I am photophobic."

In the back of her mind, Detective Amin was telling herself, *The bastard will not stand for sure, so that his height will remain unknown. But he'll die today. Please give me a reason to shoot you.*

As if he could read her mind, the dark figure said, "Before I give you a reason to shoot me, why is it that you want to meet me in person?"

"You're intelligent enough to answer that question," Detective Fielder said.

"I believe you were not able to obtain an arrest warrant for my capture. And you have not read me my Miranda rights yet." He was still under the cover of darkness.

"I don't like your sense of humor," Detective Fielder said.

"Humor is not included in my senses," the sitting figure said.

"If I see you move an inch, I'll shoot," Detective Amin said with an itchy finger on the trigger.

"Be my guest," the figure on the chair snapped.

Detective Amin saw his left hand push the table, making the chair to swivel to his right. Her aim was exact, the shoulder and then the leg.

Detective Amin pulled the trigger with two quick consecutive fires. She heard the shoulder snap and the leg bone crack. The figure fell prone to the floor.

Detective Fielder said over his headset radio, "The subject is down, repeat, the subject is down. We are approaching. The subject is not moving, but not confirmed dead."

They pointed their bright flashlight on the unmoving figure on the floor, with their guns still locked in position.

Detective Amin kicked the foot. It clanked. Inside her head she heard herself say, *What's that? A prosthetic leg?*

Detective Fielder kneeled on one of his legs, like a reverent child genuflecting in front of his creator.

He took the unwounded shoulder and turned him over. Unexpectedly, he talked, which made the detective suddenly stand and point his gun.

"Did you like my sense of humor now?" Then there was mechanical laughter, more of a shriek.

It was a mannequin.

"You bastard," Detective Fielder cursed.

The next morning, the team was again in front of their worktable. Detective Amin was not sitting; she was just standing, walking to and fro, like a hungry tiger locked in a cage waiting to be freed and attack its food.

Detective Fielder dialed the number.

The voice answered. "How did you sleep last night, Detective Fielder?"

"I lost my sleep, and I'm losing my patience, you liar."

"I am just playing the game you started, and I am just beginning to enjoy it. You set the rules; I just played it. I like free entertainment."

"So, you are entertained by killing people?"

"You really amuse me. Your partner just killed somebody last night without provocation, and you never admonished her the way you admonish me."

"Who paid you to kill the Arab president?"

"I suppose you believe in a client confidentiality policy."

"You're admitting to his murder?"

"I do not know where you got that notion. He died a natural death according to the press release."

"Yes, natural but untimely."

"Who chooses the time of anybody's death?"

"In this case, I think it is you."

"Your thinking is blasphemous."

"You don't know what I'm thinking."

"I know exactly what you are thinking. You are trying to build a rapport with me, wishing to achieve two things: to find and identify me. That is why I like talking to you. No one has really understood me, but at least you are trying to understand me."

"You are very predictable," Detective Fielder said.

"Yes. That is why I know your next move. You are basing it on the predictability of the subject's next move. That's the building block of the game you created. You know that I am going to number two, so you will block my way to number two. Then I will not move at all, and then you are blocking no one. It's entertaining, isn't it?"

"You're just a mere paid killer, a common criminal; I'll see

103

you behind bars."

"How many deaths have you actually seen? And of those you have seen, how many go to waste? I just want a small portion of those deaths."

"Do you understand that it is a crime?"

"How many people die of mosquito bites? Yet you don't blame the mosquitoes. Because you think that nature killed those people. Don't you think I am also a part of nature?"

"Nature has its own set of laws; people have their own, too, to follow."

"If nature breaks its own law, is it also punished like people are?"

"Your days are numbered; start counting," Detective Fielder said.

"It never really occurred to you that number is infinite?"

"Prepare yourself; we are getting closer."

"I know." They heard a sigh. "Your group is getting closer to being terminated."

After a month of rigorous work, Taskforce Predator was terminated. They neither located Resty nor identified him.

All members were back at their old routine jobs.

Crete Belder felt defeated; there was no more pride in him. Now, his face wore humility; arrogance was gone forever. He was young and proud because he thought he could break-in anywhere he wanted. The task force was another learning experience for him; somehow, somewhere, there would be someone more intelligent than him, and it could be far more advanced than he might have thought.

Shilin Ming was excited that she learned that most parts of an electronic item can be manipulated to serve another purpose other than the one it was made for.

For Dr. Yokohama, Detective Fielder, and Detective Amin, the search went on. They were still very active, with unwavering zeal to uncover the mask of Resty. Dr. Yokohama was commissioned to be their consultant. The paid killings continued.

Chapter 8
The Meeting

Detective Amin was very scrupulous when it came to dust and cleanliness. She always maintained that the remnant of Taskforce Predator was functioning well. She never turned off the listening device built by Shilin, Crete, and Josh.

In one corner of Starbucks, Mark Fielder and Jamila Amin drank coffee. Detective Fielder was wearily scanning the contents of the news, reading obituaries, and looking at classified ads. Detective Amin had the advertising portion, excitedly cutting coupons, and enthusiastically reading the fashion page.

Detective Amin said, "Mark, we use worms as bait, not because we like worms, but because the fish love it."

Detective Fielder said, "Believe me, Jamila, Resty knows the smell of bait." He knew exactly what she was thinking.

I believe you. But that is not my point. We will hunt what he hunts, and that's the only way we will meet him," she said. Fielder told himself in an afterthought, *My mistake.*

Detective Amin said, "If we do it, chances are, sometimes we will be too early, and that will alert him, and sometimes we will be too late and he has already taken the target."

She continued, "But with careful calculations, we might arrive there exactly on time. And we will catch him in the act of committing a crime."

Detective Fielder, in a contemplative mood, said, "It's too good to be true. And how are we going to catch him? Do you really think that he has not mapped out an escape route in case he was cornered?"

Detective Amin said, "This is a long shot, I know." She turned the page and continued. "But at least we tried. We'll be able to figure out how to catch him when he's in front of us."

"He will be careful this time. He knows that you are trigger happy." Detective Fielder turned the page.

"No, I am not. I just got emotional that time," Jamila said, and tore off a coupon.

"And how sure are you that you will not get emotional this time?" He sipped his coffee.

"I'm sure. God willing." She put down the papers, put her coffee to her lips, and then said, "We'd better hurry. That Psych doctor is waiting."

They went to Dr. Charles Meadow, a forensic psychiatrist, who specialized in serial killers.

"Detectives, this one is not a serial killer, he is a gun for hire," the doctor said. Detective Amin thought, *Oldies terminology.*

"But, doctor, just read the transcript of my conversation with him. Maybe you'll pick up something that no one else could see," Detective Fielder insisted.

"I've tried," the doctor said.

Detective Fielder was able to catch two serial killers because of Dr. Meadow's profiling, which created a picture in his mind of what the person looked like, what kind of job he had, his age group, even the clothes that he liked to wear, and what places that kind of personality would likely inhabit.

108

They were now on the freeway. "D'you like that doctor, huh?" Detective Amin said.

"Kind of," he answered.

With a bright eye, Detective Amin said, "You caught the SID killer because of him, right? The fearsome Sex in Death killer."

"Yes. And also that pedophile," Detective Fielder said, uninterested.

"Oh yes, the AMB, Abduct Molest and Bury serial killer," Detective Amin said while looking through files of music CDs. "Back home, those types of people are beheaded in public. But here, they are treated like kings. The government protects them instead of punishing them."

"We don't design the laws; we just enforce them." Detective Fielder was looking straight ahead, trying to concentrate on his driving.

"Their notorious lives were made into movies and generated big profits." Detective Amin found Shakira's *Laundry Service* and played the CD.

"They stay behind bars for life, some were electrocuted, and some had lethal injection," Detective Fielder said, tapping his fingers on the steering wheel to the tune "Whenever, Wherever."

"As humanely as possible," Detective Amin said sarcastically, swaying her head back and forth.

"We are a God-fearing people," Detective Fielder said as he honked at an absent-minded driver in front of him.

"God kills in all manners of death," she said while going through her bag.

"I don't totally believe that." Fielder looked over at the speeding, red, Corvette convertible that had just passed them.

She found what she was looking for and said, "Some became role models to the young ones who thought being bad is good. You've seen a lot of them in juvy."

"Yes. That's the period in their life that they want to create their own identity," Detective Fielder said.

He turned the left flasher on, looked at the rearview mirror, then the left side mirror, sped a little bit, and looked behind his left shoulder. There was no other car behind his left side, so he transferred to the left lane and passed the big Vons truck.

"The media make it very confusing for them." Detective Amin started retouching her lipstick with a small mirror in her hand.

"That's why there's a Film Rating Board that rates every film."

"Which make it more attractive to the underage group." She put back the mirror and lipstick in her bag. She looked at Detective Fielder's ear, thinking, *His ears are big; he has a long life,* and continued saying, "There's an ancient Arab saying that a good hunter can track down a bird just by smelling the wind."

"What do you mean?" Detective Fielder asked without looking at her.

"As far as you can remember, did you find it unusual that the place where we first found the transistor radio and the place where we found the mannequin smell the same?"

"I thought you wore the same perfume that day."

"No. I never wear that kind of perfume. In fact, it smells familiar, but I can't locate it in my mind. What perfume is it and where did I smell that before?"

"And how many people use the same perfume every day?"

"No. This one is different. Do you know that the same perfume if worn by two different persons emits two different kinds of smell?"

"I think I know a hooker just by her smell."

"And all schizophrenics smell the same."

"I think I know where this is going." He slowed a little bit as the traffic increased. "How do you plan to have a smell database?"

Detective Amin suddenly screamed, "There it is!"

Detective Fielder was startled and almost stepped on the brakes, and yelled, "Where?"

"No! Not here but right in front of our very eyes, and we don't see it."

"What is it?"

"Resty is a woman."

"You have a very good imagination."

"You're not looking. You said you thought it was me, a female smell; then a hooker, another female smell."

"I'm just keeping up with your conversation. I don't mean it was you or a hooker; I'm just trying not to be rude by not talking."

"That's good. Because a blind man can hunt better just by the smell of the prey."

"I'm not blind. I'm just stating a fact. But I don't totally disagree with you."

"You're too kind."

"No. Just tired." They entered the parking area and went to their office.

At his office, Dr. Charles Meadow was reading the complete report and the transcript. He was putting meaning into every word created. He found one pattern. The subject, called Resty, was a combination of sponge and mirror personalities, a very rare kind. First, he would absorb, then he would mirror. If I would speak to this person to see him, what I would see is just my own reflection, he would mirror my personality. This is a difficult one. Resty was just mirroring the personality of Detective Fielder.

"Let me go to the word choices," Dr. Charles Meadow said. In this kind of approach, Dr. Meadow would be able to determine the gender and age group of the speaker.

"He uses a lot of words used by sixteen-year-olds of the present time and sixteen-year-olds of the eighteenth century. He

111

uses male and female choice of words. If this person is not a very confused individual, he is a very exact person, a perfectionist. That is a trait of youth, but he is too old for that; therefore, he was not able to overcome that age level. He has not yet formed his identity in the society; identity versus identity confusion."

"He could be underage, or he doesn't want to be traced, and I concede to the second one."

"He is a master of disguise. The perfect master of disguise is somebody with multiple personalities, because he doesn't know that he is disguising himself; he really thinks and becomes the other person."

"For his killing skill, he could have trained from a master who knows no bounds to human capacity; he could have had a very rigorous training, and he could have won some medals in martial arts competitions, if he had joined one. Or it could be an inborn talent, an innermost, fully developed, animal fighting skill, inside a human body, nourished by the heart of a caring mother and protective father who would kill anyone who would want to harm his loved ones."

Three days later, Detectives Fielder and Detective Amin were reading Dr. Charles Meadow's full report. The sun set early that day. It was not five yet, and it was already dark when they finished reading.

Detective Fielder said, "What is this? It's become more difficult than before." He scratched and disarranged his hair. "Instead of narrowing our field of research, he widened it to almost everything and everyone. Oh God."

"You are blind," Detective Amin said.

"What do you see, then, that I don't see?"

"I'll give you a clue. How many people do you know with that kind of description?"

"No one."

"That's it. He is alone, unique. It's easy to spot him, because he is not like anybody else."

"That's true. But he is like a needle inside a haystack."

"Then burn the haystack, and the needle will be the only one remaining unburned."

"Yes! You are very intelligent. Elimination. And the haystack is in L.A." He went to the L.A. County map. "Where do I start?"

"No, not there. Start with ethnicity." She walked toward her listening device. There's always a static sound, sometimes faint music, sometimes unrecognizable words. She took the past twenty-four-hours record, the one that she had missed last night. In the audio room, she put the headset on and listened, fast-forwarding past every empty space. Then she heard a click. She rewound and played it again. It was very clear, and she ran screaming to Detective Fielder.

"Come! Come on! Quick! Hurry!" Detective Jamila Amin said, running toward the door. "It's a drop-off at Carl's Jr. Quick." She took out her car keys. She was driving this time.

Detective Mark Fielder followed, running out while checking his Magnum.

They arrived at Carl's Jr. A lot of people were there. Detective Amin saw the empty table with a half-eaten sandwich and a large soda, but no black bag according to what she heard on the tape. She looked at her watch, seven past five.

She told Detective Fielder, "Watch that empty table with a soda and a sandwich." Detective Fielder sat down at the opposite edge of the table.

Detective Amin went to the counter and found the cleaning boy. She showed her badge and introduced herself. "Did you see a guy with a heavy-looking black bag?"

"Oh yes I did! I'm going right now to his table. He left his trash without throwing it away," the boy said.

They walked toward Detective Fielder. When the boy started to pick up the half-eaten food, Detective Amin told the boy, "Don't touch that, please, it's mine now. Get a doggie bag, and I'll take it out."

"I can get you a new drink if you like, officer."

"No! He likes leftovers." She pointed to Detective Fielder.

They took the sandwich to Dr. Yokohama, for its saliva content. It would be fed to the Eye of the Eagle, and they would know the exact location of the one who delivered the money. The soda they were going to take to the FBI lab for a fingerprint match.

"We missed him by minutes. I should have checked that recording yesterday," Detective Amin said. She was very frustrated.

"Surely he picked up that bag. That bag is full of money. Steaming ten million dollars, and no one smelled it." She was still cursing.

"Did you notice the smell in the toilet? There was that smell again, the smell that I was telling you about. Exactly the same smell from the radio and mannequin thing."

"I did smell pee and deodorant," Detective Fielder said.

"I'm sure Resty was there," Detective Amin said.

"And he's a man, he used the men's restroom," Detective Fielder reminded her.

"We'll decide on that after we bodily search him," Detective Amin teased. "But at least we will get the delivery guy. Then we can find out who it came from."

The next day, Detective Amin was busy on the phone with the SWAT team planning the arrest of the delivery guy. He could be armed; she could not take chances, and things were getting hotter.

After she briefed the SWAT team, she and Detective Fielder went to Dr. Yokohama's laboratory. When they arrived, Dr. Yokohama greeted them and said, "Our subject is still on the move.

I'll show you; come with me."

Dr. Yokohama showed them the Earth with a moving tiny red dot. "He is probably in a car. When he stops, that will be your call." Dr. Yokohama smiled at them.

Detective Fielder's cell phone rang. He took it and went a little further outside.

When he came back, he whispered to Detective Amin, "We've got an ID. It was from the FBI."

"Oh, that's quick," Detective Amin commented.

Dr. Yokohama said, "There it is. It stopped. He is moving in small circles now. It means that he is remaining in that place. Be quick, it could be just a convenience store or whatever. He might not stay there long enough for you to catch up."

Detective Amin mobilized the SWAT team.

It was a bodybuilding club. The SWAT team surrounded the building, with snipers on the nearby rooftops.

Each team had a photo of Daniel Vargas, courtesy of the FBI files. Detective Fielder was in the lead, followed by Detective Amin, with four men from the SWAT team as cover. They entered the club. Nobody moved when the police introduced themselves.

"Mr. Daniel Vargas, come forward with your hands raised," Detective Fielder said.

Daniel Vargas stepped out from the crowd. He was a bulky man, maybe five feet ten, maybe more. It's difficult to estimate a bulky man. He was read his rights, handcuffed, and brought to the police station.

He was also released after two hours—wrong guy. His testimony was a real depiction of Resty's modus operandi. Daniel Vargas was far from scared or nervous. He was relaxed and composed, confident in what he was saying was the truth of the events: "Last week, I received a phone call, asking if I was willing to do an hour's job for a thousand dollars. I said, 'Who wouldn't?'

The next day, inside my locker, I found a black briefcase. It was locked. On the side was a white envelope with one thousand dollars in it. I took the money and deposited it in the bank to see if it was real money. The bank accepted it, and one thousand dollars was credited to my account. That night, I received another phone call. I was instructed to take the briefcase to Carl's Jr. at Normandie and Wilshire at a specific time. I would go to the counter for my order, put down the briefcase on the floor, and pay in cash. Take back the briefcase, go to any table, eat, and my job was done. That's it. Actually I was so excited that I couldn't finish my sandwich and my soda. I just left."

"Do you believe his story?" Detective Amin asked.

"I can tell when someone is lying," Detective Fielder answered.

"Me, too." Detective Amin smiled. "We've underestimated our opponent."

"You now call him an opponent?" Detective Fielder asked.

Detective Amin replied, "He became one in the course of time. He's still playing the game. And we are losing."

"He led us into several roads, but then finally we found out that road is a dead end." Detective Amin sighed. "He is trying to give us a message." She looked up at Detective Fielder and asked, "Did you pick up something?"

"Yes." He looked back at Detective Amin. "Let's play better."

The next day, Friday morning, was gloomy, and everybody was feeling lazy, looking forward to the weekend. Detective Fielder and Detective Amin were arranging their reports in their small, untidy office.

An agent knocked and entered. "Doctor Yokohama's missing. His wife called. It's good that Officer Izumi was here to talk to her. Captain Montero wants you quick."

Detective Fielder stood up and looked back at Detective Amin,

"What's their interest in Dr. Yokohama?"

The agent said, "You know his inventions. We're not able to give him the proper protection that he and his inventions need. We thought they wouldn't work."

"You're telling me that there were other parties who knew about his inventions?" Detective Fielder asked.

"Yes," the agent was saying while almost running back to Captain Montero's office.

"It's our fault," Detective Amin said.

Detective Fielder was almost running to the captain's office. Captain Montero, who had just finished talking with the director of the FBI, was now busy on the phone talking to the director of the CIA.

Captain Montero put down the phone and said, "It's too late. The information leaked when Doctor Yokohama was using the satellite of a private company. Of course, it was very interesting, but the government bureaucracy slowed everything. Someone discovered the unprotected gold mine, Doctor Yokohama's inventions," he said, exhausted from the recent unforeseen event.

"Three agencies are now involved to find Dr. Yokohama. If he was taken by and into another country, the doctor could be coerced to swear allegiance to that country, become a citizen, and become a government property. That could be the worst scenario, and it cannot be allowed. It could mean another war," Captain Montero said.

Detective Amin said, "I think he was taken by a big company, planning to market the product on their own."

"Or he could be in the hands of a terrorist organization now." Detective Fielder caught up with her.

One agent came in and said, "According to the FBI report, the doctor could still be in the country."

Detective Fielder and Detective Amin stood up and said,

117

"We're going to his laboratory." They talked to Dr. Yokohama's assistant, Bryanna Johanson.

They told Bryanna what happened, that Dr. Yokohama had disappeared.

"Surely you can locate him, right?" Detective Fielder asked.

Bryanna looked straight at him. "Yes. Of course. That was the first test given to me by the doctor: to locate him, using his dandruff." She walked inside and toward her panel of keyboards and monitors.

In less than an hour, Bryanna was able to locate the doctor. He was in a remote, old, abandoned ranch that had no neighbors in Sylmar, Los Angeles County.

"There he is," Detective Amin said, excited.

"Wait!" Bryanna said. "Let me scan that place in my little, improved scanner." She hit several keys, and different angles of the place appeared, like rotating a small house in her hands and examining it from the top, sides, and below, a three-dimensional view.

Bryanna focused the image. "There he is. Twenty-five feet below the ground. It could be a basement or a dungeon, or a tunnel."

"Even if we have a search warrant, we will not be able to find the doctor in there. Surely there's a secret passage concealed somewhere that's impossible to find by outsider."

Bryanna was still busy with the keyboard. "Don't worry, he's alone. Let me put a trace on the doctor's falling debris en route to his current location." A multitude of green dots appeared connected by red lines from the Earth's surface down to the dungeon in three dimensions.

She printed it, handed it over to Detective Fielder, and said, "You now have a map of the place; I hope you can locate the doctor when you get there. Tell me if I can be of any more help to you."

"No, thank you. This is more than enough." Detective Fielder and Detective Amin almost ran out of the laboratory.

While Fielder was busy driving and talking to Captain Montero on his cell phone, Amin was also busy setting up the SWAT team for a possible armed encounter, in case the place was protected by an unseen, private army hiding somewhere and monitoring the activities. She could not take chances.

They reached the place; it was a broad, uninhabited, grass field. At the center was an old, rotting, wooden structure. There was nothing inside the old structure. Detective Fielder consulted the map that Bryanna printed. He found on the ground a concealed, wooden trapdoor. With his gun in his right hand and with the SWAT team on the ready, full of bright Maglites, he opened the door. It was an opening to a long staircase going down, very deep and very dark. When they reached the bottom, there was Dr. Yokohama, bound to a chair. His blindfold hung loosely on his neck.

Dr. Yokohama was rescued without incident, but there was no one to charge with his kidnapping. Nobody owned the place, and Dr. Yokohama could not remember a face or even a voice.

The doctor said that he had been abducted at gunpoint from the laboratory's parking lot, blindfolded, and the only time his blindfold was removed was when he was in a very dark room, bound and seated on a heavy chair. From what he overheard, he was due to be transported tonight, but he was rescued earlier. This was another dead end. It was Friday night.

On Monday, the doctor did not come to work, a very strange thing to happen. No one had a clue; no call, no show, which was very unlike him. Detective Amin called his house. No one answered the phone. When no one was able to locate him by noon, everyone panicked.

Bryanna used the data that she had used to trace Dr. Yokohama using the "Eye of the Eagle" but he could not be traced using any of the laboratory's equipment. All the data available about him and his family had vanished.

On top of Bryanna's table was a piece of paper with printed symbols. Handing it over to Detective Amin she said, "Do you think this has something to do with his disappearance?"

"Let me look at it." Detective Amin took the paper with the symbols:

❀〰♏◲ ◆☐☐& ◯◲ ◆♓⚒♏ ♋■♎ ◯◲
♍〰♓●♌☐♏■ ♋◆ ♓■◆◆☐♋■♍♏ ⚔☐☐ ◯◲
♍☐☐☐♏♍♋◆♓☐■

Detective Amin said, "These are not symbols; they are actual words in another Microsoft Word font."

She sat down at the nearest terminal, logged in and opened the Word program. She typed the alphabet from A to Z, highlighted it and started changing the fonts. It was a Wingdings font. She picked up all the symbols one by one, according to their arrangement. Finally, this was the message: "They took my wife and my children as insurance for my cooperation."

Chapter 9
The Ordeal of Dr. Yokohama

On the day that Dr. Yokohama was abducted, the message was clear. The man in the black mask clearly told the doctor, "This kidnapping is just a diversion and a test. If your equipment really works, your people would be able to rescue you without difficulty. On the day that you are rescued, your wife and two children will be with us. Remove all the data, so that no one can trace you and your family. Any single hint that they are coming near to us, and we will kill your family."

The man faced the doctor and gave him the instructions, "Commit this number to memory." The man handed him a piece of paper with a phone number, and after few seconds, he took it back and burned it with a cigarette lighter. "Call that number on Friday night at ten. We will give you the instructions, so that we can pick you up."

Dr. Yokohama was now in an unknown laboratory, with more sophisticated equipment necessary to perfect his inventions, the Eye of the Eagle and the Golden Eye. He was happy that he would be able to perfect his inventions, a great advantage to mankind to stop the crime that he dreaded, although that crime was now being perpetrated against him. He was also sad that after he perfected his inventions, he did not know if he would live to see his family. He had to find a way to escape, or at least save his family. He could not contact Detective Fielder, and even if he could, he did not know where he or his family was. There was only one chance to save his family: the Paid Killer, Resty. He was the only one who could possibly be contacted without being detected.

The next day, Saturday morning, he drank black coffee. He was sitting comfortably until noon, pretending to be relaxed and not worried. The masked man came to him and asked. "Why are you not working on the project?"

"I'm bored to death."

"What entertainment do you wish?"

He sipped his now-cold coffee. "What I need is a transistor radio, I cannot work without it. I listen to my favorite programs while I am working. I do talk with the radio during the program, some people think that I am crazy doing that."

The man laughed and said, "It will be here soon."

After a couple of hours, the masked man came in with a big transistor radio with a CD and cassette player, and some music CDs and tapes.

"When I am at work, I do not want to be disturbed," he said and took the radio inside the laboratory.

He thought, *It was good that I had a chance to study how it works.* He was referring to how Resty modified the transistor radio.

The laboratory had a special design. The guards can see the face of Dr. Yokohama, but they could not see what he was doing. The masked man said that this was Magnus's design. He said, "Magnus told me, 'Do not let others do unto you, what you have done unto them.'" He was referring to the spies planted in the doctor's laboratory.

A three-man ring of industrial spies were sent to work at Dr. Yokohama's laboratory after Senator Magnus's technical adviser told him of the satellite activities being done in sector twenty-five northeast, the portion that the doctor was leasing. The spies were able to deliver the complete project study of Dr. Yokohama, the Eye of the Eagle and the Golden Eye.

Magnus saw the potential. He had the power and the means. He told himself, *This is the key to the door that I want to enter, the presidency.*

Last Sunday evening, Senator Magnus was in his study.

Magnus, in his dreamy speech, with one audience, Bart, the masked man, said, "Bart, look at me, look at my eyes." Magnus paused for a second and continued. "You are now looking at the eyes of the future president of the United States of America." Magnus was an ambitious senator.

"I will start my political campaign." He gestured to the wall as if he was reading something written on it. "Missing persons are a thing of the past. I am Magnus, your key to a safe way of life and freedom from fear, a kind of freedom that has never been given by any president to his own people.

"Here's my plan. My company will be the sole owner of this technology. Any agency, or individual, here or abroad, could have access to the Eye of the Eagle. A discount can be arranged for any voter as a public show of my sincere service to them. The name will be changed to the Eye of the Magnus." Then he laughed an evil laugh of victory.

"The Golden Eye will also have a new name; it will be called Magnus View." He faced Bart and said, "The work of the doctor should be extremely guarded. No one from the viewing room should see what he's doing."

"Don't worry, Magnus; he is completely isolated. I am the only one allowed to enter the laboratory. There is a laser that I am the only one who knows the code to turn it off. Anybody who passes it will be fried extremely well done." He laughed like a small boy who just got an ice cream, and continued, "He talks only to his transistor radio."

Magnus suddenly stopped, terrified and shouted, "What? A radio? Are you that stupid, Bart?"

"No! No, no, Magnus. I personally owned that old radio and that's the one I gave him," Bart said defensively.

"When will your brain grow? The doctor can modify it and can talk to the outside world, whenever he likes. Don't you know that a seven-year-old boy can make a transistor radio where that doctor came from?" Exasperated, Magnus sat down.

"I just don't know how much damage you already have done to my dreams," he continued. "When did you give it to him?"

"Yesterday."

"Take it back immediately. Bring me the records of all the sounds that came from that laboratory from the time you gave him that radio."

Bart immediately went to the laboratory, decoded the laser, took out the doctor, and sent him to another holding room with the guards. "Search him, a whole body search for anything metallic or glass-like, anything that is not normally part of the body, and give it to me."

The guards took the doctor out. First he was placed in a scanner and x-ray. Then he was told to take off all his clothing. There was someone assigned to search the clothing and someone assigned for a body search. The doctor thought, *They don't know that what they are looking for is inside my brain, and it is invisible; it is knowledge.* After the search, the doctor was brought back to his room.

"Sorry, no radio is allowed in your room," Bart said. He went outside and closed the door behind him.

Last night, the doctor had activated Resty's frequency. It was not that difficult to access it once you have done it more than three times. Then he said, "I need your services."

An eerie sound penetrated the doctor's ears, then a modulated voice, "Gooood morniiiing, dear listeners. This is your favorite dedication and service station. Any callers? Do you want to dedicate a song to your loved ones? Here is our program, to whom and what do you like to dedicate?"

Dr. Yokohama immediately recognized the voice of the Paid Killer in another world. He was so surprised that Resty was talking in symbols, as if he knew that somebody was listening and he wanted the doctor to talk in symbols, too.

"I want to dedicate a song to my wife and kids. The song 'My Fair Share,' the love theme from One on One, nineteen seventy-seven, lyrics by Paul Williams, music by Charles Fox," the doctor said happily.

There was the sound of a ringing phone from the radio, then static and the voice again of Resty. "We have a caller, 'Killing Me Softly With His Song' for his wife and girls. And the music started. Resty's fading voice said, "Don't forget, listeners, I'll be back on Tuesday night. Don't forget your gifts to your wife and kids tonight, folks, before you go home." And the music went on and on.

The doctor knew that that it was a signal from Resty that he should turn off the radio or transfer to another station, and he did. Then he located the doctor's family and delivered the message back to him.

Dr. Yokohama was able to locate his family. He immediately turned the frequency to Resty's RF and delivered the message. He was singing a song, ". . . I have seen the dove with her two chicks. Forty-eighth Street, the far corner mansion, under the basement at the east corner. I'll pay you with my life just to get the dove and its babies. Tum tum turum tum." He worked continuously that night. The guards were getting bored and sleepy.

Monday late evening, Bart went to the senator's office,

bringing the recordings. Magnus was pacing his large office, overlooking the view of the ocean. "Is there a problem, Senator?" Bart asked.

"I don't know yet. There were two detectives nosing around the satellite company. They were investigating the disappearance of the doctor. Obviously, the company would be their first place to look. The doctor leased the services of the satellite for his project. And those detectives know that."

"But they don't have anything."

"Nothing. But we don't know what they are looking for and what they have seen already."

"What do you want me to do then?"

"Nothing. Just give me that and go back to your work."

After two hours, the senator told his secretary that if something came up, he should not be disturbed, and he would be back in the office tomorrow morning.

Magnus called Bart on his way. "Bart, go to the library of the safe house right now. I'll meet you there."

The safe house was the senator's private property. It was guarded by well-trained ex-Marines looking for an easy job with higher pay. Magnus paid them well for maximum security to his satisfaction. The safe house had several unlisted telephone lines, secret passages, and a well-guarded basement where Dr. Yokohama's wife and children were being held.

In the library, Magnus was showing the transcript to Bart. "Look, Bart. With whomever the doctor was talking, they were talking in codes. The one he was talking to already knew where the doctor was. He wants the doctor to locate the wife and kids tonight. Then on Tuesday, that's the day that they'll attack to rescue the doctor and the wife and kids."

Bart was amazed and asked, "Magnus, how did you come to that conclusion?"

"I don't know if you really didn't listen to the recording before you gave it to me, or did you?"

"You know I'll not lie to you. Of course I did."

"What did you get then?"

"I know that kind of program. I'm familiar with that. That's like *Sleepless in Seattle*. Tom Hanks and Meg Ryan."

"This one's not like that. The doctor said, 'I need your services.' Then the other one answered in coded phrases, like what kind of service do you want. Then the doctor said that his wife and children are missing and he wants them rescued, from the theme song, 'My Fair Share.' Oh you have to know that song to understand."

"And then 'Killing Me Softly' means he already got the message, turn off your radio now. It's coded. That's why you don't understand it. Anyway, you're useful to me in another way. I don't want to take chances; this is the ultimate success that will lead me to the seat of the presidency. Get me the phone number of that assassin who killed the yakuza drug lords. I know he was hired by that rival Italian drug lord Don Victorini. And we still have a day to mobilize our trap for the attack on Tuesday night. We will set up an ambush."

"Magnus, why do you need the number of that assassin?"

"I don't want to have any connection with the death of those two detectives who came to the satellite station this morning. Detective Mark Fielder and that female detective, Detective Jamila something. I think they know where to look. Sometimes I hate people who know how to do their jobs."

Bart made a few phone calls before he got Resty's number. Then Senator Magnus called his chief of security to come to the library. Bart briefed the chief of security about a possible attack on Tuesday. The ambush should be ready by morning. The three of them spent the other three hours planning and making several phone calls.

The chief of security dispatched five of his best, including himself, to go outside and recruit extra hands for the ambush.

Before they finally dispersed, the last call to be made was the call to Resty. Senator Magnus dialed the number. The first was a single ring, and then an electronic voice message: *The number you dialed is not a working number.* He signaled to Bart, and Bart signaled to dial again. He dialed a second time. Another electronic message: *We're sorry, the number is not complete as dialed, please check the number and dial again.* Bart made the gesture to continue dialing. He dialed a third time, there was a long dial tone, and then it went dead. The fourth time he dialed, the phone rang.

"How can I be of service to you?"

"Two persons need to be killed ASAP."

"And who might they be?"

"Detective Mark Fielder and Detective Jamila Amin."

"Sounds like a difficult target."

Twenty million each."

"Half now, nonrefundable. The other half after the job."

"You want it now? And nonrefundable? But suppose you don't succeed?"

"Why call me then?"

"You have the sound of arrogance. You don't even know who you are talking to."

"I'm not interested in who you are."

"You don't even know that I can put you away forever . . ."

"Stop right there! The only reason that you are alive today is just because no one has yet put a price on your head. But when someone does, I will look at you as just simple useless dead meat. Do you want the deal or not?"

"Of course I want it. You . . ."

"Prepare the money now and save your speech for your next

Senate meeting." The line went dead.

Senator Magnus was shocked. Then he shouted, "Baaarrrt!"

"Yes, Magnus?"

"I was told that nobody knows this phone. I was identified by that bastard. He knows me."

"I was told he's that good. Once you call him, he knows you at once. Wait for a few minutes. He will call back for the instructions where and how we are going to deliver the money."

"Do you have the cash?"

"Yes. That's why I went out to the cash vault. I heard you promise that prick."

After ten minutes, Resty called back with instructions on how and where to deliver the money.

After they dispersed, they all went home with peaceful minds that everything would be taken care of, and they could all sleep in tranquility.

Monday night.

Resty in a black suit with a masked face, arrived at the gate with a short-handled sledgehammer. Resty hammered the hinges of the window of the guard house; he knew that the locked side would not open in one hit, but the hinges would. It snapped open. He jumped inside and hit the startled guard with the hammer. The guard fell. All was quiet after that one quick *braaang* sound.

Resty swiftly ran toward the door of the mansion. Two guards saw his approach and they opened fire toward Resty. For Resty, guns were the most stupid weapons invented by men. A bullet goes in a straight line. Once you were off that line, the bullet had no capability to curve to follow the target. Just look where the nose was pointing and stay away from that point; it was that easy for Resty. In just a few swift steps, the head of one guard was hammered down, and instantly Resty swung his body, lifting a leg upward, the heel of his shoe connecting to the jaw of the other guard, with an impact so strong that the guard's cervical spine snapped. The two guards were down, never to stand again.

One of the dead guards had the door key. Resty had committed to memory the map of the mansion from the song invented by Dr. Yokohama. Resty had to kill every combatant in the mansion; he couldn't risk keeping anyone alive while taking away the wife and two kids.

A sledgehammer and a foot versus guns and knives. For Resty, knives were better than guns. If a knife is handled swiftly, it follows the target wherever it goes; bullets don't have that capability.

Four guards approached Resty from two sides firing their guns to no avail. Resty knew where the bullets were going, and he swiftly moved out of the target area and toward the two. Resty jumped, his body swung horizontally, the sledgehammer hit the guard's chest, throwing him to the wall with a ruptured heart muscle, an instant painful death ten times more lethal than a massive cardiac arrest. Resty's foot hit the neck of the other guard, occluded the windpipe, producing a deadly esophageal spasm that trapped all the air in the lungs with no way for the air to come in or out. The guard desperately held his throat and dropped to the floor with a few seconds to hang onto his dear life. Resty dropped to the floor, squatted, picked up a handgun in his left hand, and simply shot the other two targets. Resty was sorry for the two guards who were not quick enough to stay away from the bullets speeding toward their foreheads; they were just incidental targets.

Resty hung the sledgehammer on his waist, picked up another two handguns putting in fresh clips. He walked swiftly toward the hallway and went down to the basement. Two guards appeared with machine guns, but before they were able to point the weapons toward the intruder, their skulls had already been crushed by the impact of the bullets coming from Resty's left and right handguns.

Resty ran swiftly toward the end of the hallway, dropping to the floor sideways. He knew he would be welcomed by sprays of bullets from the other side of the corner.

A few seconds earlier, the other two guards saw their comrades fall to the ground spraying their machine pistols upward to the walls and ceiling, breaking some lamps on their way down, splattering blood and brain matter on the walls.

They got ready in firing positions for the intruder to appear. Something swiftly appeared from down on the floor, out of accurate firing range. They pointed their guns, but it was too late, bullets were already in front of their eyes. Then all of a sudden, there was pain and numbness, then bright nothingness.

Resty saw the last two guards fall. The door had no ordinary locks. It was electronically operated; the combination was known maybe to only few people. He took out a handgun with a silencer and three more clips from the guard's holster and put them in his waist.

Resty pulled out the sledgehammer. He had to disconnect the steel door from the concrete. With four full swings, the metal door disconnected from the concrete, and one last strong hit made the heavy door fell to the floor. Resty saw three fearful faces in a corner of the room.

"*Moshi moshi*, Doctor Yokohama sent me to pick you up. Come quickly." In the garage, they saw several cars: a Hummer, a Jaguar, a Lotus, an Alfa Romeo, a Corvette, and a Mustang. All the keys were hanging on the key hooks on the wall near the door. He took the key of the Hummer. He held it on the edge only, using the point of a small knife, and he pressed the unlock button twice and said to Mrs. Yokohama and kids, "Go in quickly!" They entered the backseat. Resty suddenly locked the doors. The family panicked and started pushing and hitting the windows and the back of the front seat. Resty pushed the unlock button again and opened the door. "That's too big. Let's get in a smaller car." Resty returned the key of the Hummer and took the Mustang.

In few minutes, they were already in front of the deserted area where the doctor was being held captive. On the roof there were three small dish antennae: one black and two silver.

The chicken wire fence had a high voltage electric current, very visible from the warning signs. He put out a long, black, insulated wire and connected it from one pole to the next pole. Then with his homemade sulfuric acid spray, he sprayed it in one straight line from top to bottom. No breach of security appeared from the inside monitor because it was wired together.

He kept the engine running and gave strict instructions to the three not to move and to wait for him and the doctor to come out.

Inside the building, the screen of the radar monitor showed the approaching vehicle, and then it stopped on one side of the premises.

"Ken, will you check out what that car's doing outside the premises."

"You know that it's dark in that part. Maybe two lovers are away from home and have no money for a motel."

"Anyway, check it out."

Ken stood up, grunting. "Okay, sir."

He went out of the hallway toward the door. He opened it and lazily walked out. On his first step outside, he suddenly felt a strong grip on his throat. His eyes bulged, everything was red, he could not move, but he could feel his body quivering. The red became black, and he remembered no more.

Resty put the limp body on the ground, took the dead guard's cell phone, and put it in his pocket. With a swift step toward the hallway, he took out the two silenced pistols in both hands. He went straight to the viewing room, instantly killing the four guards with one bullet each into their skulls. The doctor could not be seen inside the laboratory; he was in his sleeping room. He saw the laser toward the holding room. He pumped several bullets in each side. The laser malfunctioned, and the lights went off.

He took out the sledgehammer and hit the hinges near the wall. The door fell down. Resty peeked in and called, "Doctor, come quickly."

Dr. Yokohama was half-asleep when he heard the loud crash, and a familiar voice called to him. He immediately stood up and looked out. He saw a slim black figure, and thought, *My God, this is the Paid Killer in person.*

Resty said, "Come quick, your wife and children are waiting for you." Resty ran, and the doctor followed.

When he saw his family inside the car, he ran and embraced them while tears were welling out from his eyes, as he told his wife and kids in Japanese, "I thought I would never see you again. I never expected that we would see each other again."

While driving away, Resty made a short phone call. "Sweetie pie, I have a family here. Very important: No one should know about them until I tell you so. Is that clear?" He paused for few seconds and said, "We'll be there in a few minutes." He never dialed anything. He threw the cell phone outside the window, crushing it into tiny pieces of dust along the way.

They arrived on a dark private road in front of a high metal gate made of brass bars, a shining brass ball on top of each one.

"Someone will let you in; you'll be good. I'll inform Detective Mark Fielder that you are safe. Don't call anyone until your hostess tells you so. The secrecy of your whereabouts is very important for the time being."

"We understand," Dr. Yokohama said. "I just don't know how to thank you."

"You promised me you will pay me with your life," Resty

said. "I don't need your life, but I could use your services once in a while."

"Anytime; just tell me, and I am at your service."

"Go now; someone's waiting for you."

Dr. Yokohama went down the road, followed by his wife and two kids. They went in front of the high gate, and the Mustang sped away. The gate opened, and the electronic voice from the intercom said, "Welcome to Lightston Mansion. You may enter. Approach the main door and you shall be received."

While walking toward the Mansion, Toshimi, the seven-year-old boy asked, "Dad, who's the king who lives here?"

"There's no king in here."

"Isn't it a king who lives in a castle?"

"Yes, but this is not a castle."

"It looks like one."

"When we're inside, don't ask any questions. Don't talk unless you're asked. Remember that, okay?"

"Okay, Daddy," Akira, the four-year-old daughter said.

They approached a highly ornamented, very large door. An elderly man opened the door and welcomed them. They saw a lady in front of the piano, slightly singing with the tune. She had lustrous, long, flowing, dark brown hair.

"Madam, here are your guests."

She stopped playing, looked back smiling, stood up, and went to welcome them.

"My name is Adelin. I'm your hostess." She led them into the dining area.

"Come please, the dining table's ready. You must be hungry."

"Please forgive us; to be honest with you, we're starving."

"Oh, don't worry about it."

They voraciously attacked the dining table. Toshimi had food in his right and left hands, alternately putting it in his mouth, both cheeks were bulging and chewing at the same time. Akira put a lot of colorful food in her plate and one by one put anything that would fit into her small mouth. Hunger was just a secondary factor, the feeling of relief and safety was first, which made them so excited, happily eating together as a family.

At two in the morning, Detective Fielder was awakened by the sudden loud ringing of his phone. He was startled and took the phone and said in the mouthpiece, "This better be good!"

"I'm afraid not." It was Detective Amin.

"Someone put a price on our heads."

"What?"

Detective Amin said, "I picked it up while the monitor was on Resty's frequency."

"Do you know from where?"

She told him everything she heard.

"Are you scared?" Mark asked.

"In our kind of work, nothing can scare me anymore. We're always a target, twenty-four seven, and you know it well."

"How long do we have?"

"Thirty-six hours," Jamila said.

"What shall we do?"

"This is our best chance. We don't need to find him anymore; he'll find us wherever we are."

"We can set up a trap," Mark said loudly.

"You're more intelligent than I thought."

"Stop the sarcasm, please." Mark mellowed.

"I'm just excited at this opportunity."

"See you first thing in the morning," Mark said, and hung up the phone, but sleep never came back. He went to make coffee.

He remembered something: *The abduction of the poor Dr. Yokohama and his family. They are my first priority.*

He stood up and told himself, *Yes, the poor doctor and his family have been abducted. I almost forgot. So, Resty's working for the senator. He abducted the poor doctor. And he's after me and Jamila.* He could not sleep anymore. He went to his computer, while making some phone calls to the FBI tracking system department. He would track down the power source of the satellite system where the doctor rented his tracking device; he wanted to see if it would lead to the senator.

On Tuesday, at five in the morning, Senator Magnus was awakened by the sudden ringing of his secured phone, coming from the safe house. When he saw it, he thought, *Oh, good news. The troops are early for the ambush today or maybe tonight.*

Magnus picked up the phone. "Yes, Bart? Give the troops a good breakfast."

"Yes, Magnus, bah, bah . . . but . . . but . . ."

"But what?"

"The wife and the kids are gone."

"Whaaat? Get the doctor immediately!"

"He's gone, too."

"Who's the traitor? Who did this to us? Find the survivor; he's the traitor!"

"No survivors, Magnus. All are dead." He sighed deeply. "What shall I tell the police?"

"You're not telling them a single word. That's their work to find out."

Detective Fielder went to his office at seven-thirty in the morning, expecting to be early, but Detective Amin was already there taking her strong-smelling Arabic coffee.

"You're early," Detective Fielder said to Detective Amin.

"I'm always early." She looked up. "Oh, it's because of my morning prayers, before dawn."

"What's up, then?"

"Look at this computer printout. It is so intricate, as intricate

136

as the Bible story."

"And what d'you know about the Bible? It's plain and simple, no intricacies there."

"When they ran out of wine in the wedding in Cana, where did the servants go?"

"To Mary."

"When the satellite had a problem with jurisdiction, where did the CEO go for approval?"

"To whom?"

"To Senator Magnus."

"How do you relate that to Mary?"

"I don't know if you're just playing stupid. But I understand you. It's faith versus fact." She handed him the transcript. "You put your faith too much in your senator; that's why you're blinded by the fact. Like the intricate Bible story, the servants would never go to a mother of a guest if they run out of wine, or else the groom will suffer town humiliation from the gossipers; of course they would go to the mother of the groom. But the senator does not want to be identified. So the Bible did not identify the groom. Did you understand that?"

"Our lives are in danger," Mark said.

An agent came rushing in without knocking. "Multiple homicides, it's a massacre at Senator Magnus's manor and a communications lab in Simi Valley. They said it's like a war zone."

Both stood up and ran outside toward the parking lot to their car. When they arrived, the coroner was already there, the CSI, the paramedics, and Captain Montero.

After the badge waving and greetings, they found familiar faces inside, already doing their work. Detective Amin walked slowly, as if tracing something.

"What are you doing?" asked Detective Fielder.

"I'm re-enacting the scene, from the time the attackers came in, up to where they reached before they backed out."

"And then?"

"Then I'll be able to tell why this estate has been attacked in the first place." She pointed to the wall. "Do you know how much a Paul Cézanne painting is?"

"No. Maybe twenty to thirty dollars at Ross."

"Let's say in the neighborhood of eighty million dollars."

"So the purpose of the attack was not burglary?"

"You're getting smarter," Detective Amin said.

"What's in this estate that it was attacked?"

"That's what everybody's trying to find out."

"I was just talking to myself."

"You mean you are thinking out loud?"

"Yes," Mark said.

"Next time, think quietly. They can hear your thoughts." Detective Amin pointed to the knights in metal suits on both sides of the hallway.

They went through the killing lines, until they reached the door leading to the basement. Inside the basement, Detective Amin traced the logical position of the attackers, by means of the shell casings found and their positions, until they reached the broken door. Inside the small room, Detective Amin picked up a tiny doll, made of torn cloth.

"A small girl was crying, and the mother tore her skirt, made it into a doll, gave it to her, and the girl stopped crying," Jamila said.

"Are you thinking out loud, too?" Mark said, trying to get even.

"No. I'm trying to tell you that Doctor Yokohama and his family were here. They were abducted from the abductors," Jamila said.

"We better be on our way to Simi Valley now."

"We better be."

They walked fast to their car. When they reached the communications laboratory, the paramedics were starting to move the bodies toward their ambulances. The detectives waved their badges at the uniformed police officers, and they entered the building.

A uniformed police officer was putting a large radio-cassette recorder into a plastic bag. Detective Fielder asked, "Where're you taking that?"

"Crime lab, sector five."

"Thanks." Detective Fielder took out his cell phone and dialed a number.

A voice answered him from the other line. "Sector five, how can I help you?"

"May I speak with Tony, please? This is Detective Mark Fielder."

"Okey dokey! Tony, phone for you, it's Detective Fielder."

"Hi, it's Tony."

"Hi, buddy!"

"Hi Mark, what can I do for you?"

"You'll receive a radio-cassette recorder from a crime scene. I want you to look for alterations of the internal design, circuitry and parts."

"Gotcha! I'll give you a call."

"Thanks." He hung up and put his cell phone back in its cradle at his waist.

He looked at Detective Amin and said, "We've got at least twenty-eight hours more to live."

"The senator owns both war zones," Detective Amin said.

"In my analysis, both war zones were not attacked by a group of attackers, but by one person only, and by the same person," Detective Mark Fielder concluded.

Detective Amin caught up. "Yes, because there was no mess

139

from the attacker, only from those dead guards."

Mark said, "Not only that, the style of opening the doors, the killing of the front liners, not taking anything of value and just taking out the Yokohama family. They were separated. Dr. Yokohama was in the communications lab, and the family was in the mansion. I didn't realize at first that the doctor serves another purpose."

"The doctor was coerced to do something in exchange for the safety of his family."

"Exactly," Mark said, and continued. "Where are those communications between the senator and Resty?"

"It is already at Captain Montero's office. He's going to the D.A.'s Office for an arrest warrant," Jamila said.

"How can we stop Resty from killing us . . . just in case?" Mark looked at Jamila.

Jamila looked back. "You're scared, aren't you?"

"Who wouldn't be?" Mark looked outside the window and continued. "Haven't you seen those guards, how they were taken out without difficulty?"

Jamila was quiet. Mark continued. "And did you recognize that some of those guards were once members of the most elite fighting machine of the U.S. Marines and Navy SEALs?"

"Yes, I've seen their marks," Jamila said. "I thought we were going to set up a trap?"

"He's smart enough to smell a trap," Mark said.

"If we stay away from each other, he will not be able to get the deadline, but each of us is vulnerable alone," Jamila said. "But if we stay together, maybe we can devise a strategy to defeat him."

"Maybe I can just booby-trap myself, embrace him, and explode." Mark felt defeated this time.

"Don't be such a fool, Detective Mark Fielder," Jamila said. "I have a plan."

"And what is that?"

"We stay on the top floor of our building, in one of the secured rooms, lock all doors, watch TV, drink coffee, and wait till he comes."

"You mean, put ourselves in jail."

"No! That is the trap. He has no way out. We'll tell the captain our plan; he'll post several plainclothes around the vicinity, sharpshooters on top of other high-rise buildings. You know the drill."

"Let's get going."

The next day, fingerprints of the missing Mrs. Yokohama and the two kids were found all over inside the Hummer of Senator Magnus. The head of security for the senator was invited for questioning.

At nine in the evening, the previous shift policemen were getting off, and the new shift was coming in. Lieutenant McDowell was shouting, "Alvarez! Where's that hooker that I arrested earlier?"

Alvarez looked up. "I saw her sitting on that bench, sir," he said pointing to his left. "Maybe she went to the bathroom or something."

They never found the hooker again. Resty was at work inside the police headquarters where he discovered the trap plan, and it excited him to jump into it. This was just a game for him. Trap his victims in their own trap.

Resty was now in a police uniform, a young and innocent-looking neophyte who collated reports. He could go anywhere in the building with no one taking a second look. He looked like every other new graduate. He knew exactly where his two targets would be spending their time tonight. Then he vanished between the walls and between floors and ceilings and started setting up a trap within a trap.

Detective Mark Fielder and Detective Amin were watching the news. Senator Magnus had just been arrested minutes ago. They both stood up, maybe to listen better or to feel more involved because of their knowledge of the case. Detective Amin felt that she was a part of his capture. The news said that he had hired someone to kill two police officers, her and Detective Mark Fielder.

But before she could say anything, a sharp and tiny burning sensation tightened around her neck and pulled her up. Her first reflex was to hold on to that something that was pulling her up or she would be strangled to death. She looked at Mark; he was in the same situation as she was. A tiny and very strong nylon fishing cord was around Mark's neck, pulling him upward. His face was so red, his eyes started to bulge, and so were hers.

A black figure jumped down from the ceiling with the fluidity of an Olympic gymnast. She knew that this was Resty, in person, and she had never imagined that her life would end this way.

Resty said, "I was paid in half, so I will also half kill you both." He pointed to the TV. "I suppose you know it all; I will never be paid in full." With a swift swing of Resty's blade, the nylon cords were cut, and the two detectives fell to the floor, gasping for air. Resty ran to the window.

Mark was quick to grab the head cover of the masked killer. While Jamila was quick with her gun to shoot Resty. For an instant, Mark saw his face, a face he would never forget as long as he lived.

Jamila shot the target, three consecutive rounds, straight to the chest. But Resty fell backward, and the bullets missed. Resty's left foot kicked upward the hand of Mark with the black headgear, and Resty grabbed it, leaving no souvenir for the detectives.

Resty fell from the eighteenth floor of the building. The two detectives were sure what to expect on the pavement—another mess for the coroner. But at least a fingerprint or a dental record or even DNA would give them a positive identification of Resty, the Paid Killer. May he rest in peace.

They ran out to the elevator. They reached the street level and went straight to where Resty fell. Expecting a crowd of onlookers, they saw nothing out of the ordinary. No mangled body on the pavement. They looked upward; some passersby looked upward to the sky or to the building. Nothing unusual; the building was just flat glass that reflected the lights of different moving colors.

They looked at each other, thinking, *Did he fly?*

Mark spoke. "I saw his face; I can describe it to our sketch artist. We'll distribute his picture to all the police forces and the media until we catch him."

Inside a bathroom stall in the opposite building, Resty was removing the face that Mark saw. Lustrous, flowing, light brown long hair bounced down below her shoulders, and she smiled in front of the mirror while arranging her clothes and fixing her lipstick, and walked out.

The next day, Detective Fielder was in his office with the strong smell of Arabic coffee, massaging his painful neck while watching the TV with the picture of the Paid Killer.

The phone rang. He picked up. "Hello?"

"Detective Fielder? This is Doctor Yokohama."

The voice was so familiar. Excited, he shouted, "Jamila! Doctor Yokohama's alive."

Part III

Chapter 1
France

The Eiffel Tower was like a proud giant looking over his vast kingdom with little creatures in it. The early morning was still chilly; the sun had just started to peek along the cloudless horizon.

Outside the tent of the traveling international circus performers, a couple was quietly talking over their breakfast table.

Natasha, the acrobatic dancer, pointed something out to her husband Anatoly, the vanishing magician.

"Look at this news," she said spreading the newspaper on the table. "This is the latest." Reading loudly, "A U.S. senator has been indicted, connected to the kidnapping of a scientist and his family, who are still missing at this time, and the attempted assassination of two celebrated police officers. Their police training and tactics saved them."

She looked at him and continued, "You know my hobbies. Since high school, I have collected bizarre things from the newspaper. When we were recuperating at the rehab center, I started saving all these clippings again. Five years ago, one of my trademarks appeared in the *Los Angeles Times*. A circus manager found hanging by a fishing line from the high wire of his own tent.

But a month before that, I cut out a certain bizarre news item about modern cannibalism. An old abandoned house in a remote place in Texas was found with a lot of cooked bodies in giant cookware. Then a year ago, one of my other trademarks appeared again. A Christian pastor bled to death from a severed sexual organ who was later found to be a serial rapist/killer of young girls, according to the *Los Angeles Times*. Then another one, a man found hanging upside down in an alleyway with all his guts hanging down to the dirt and flies swarming and hatching their maggots. Another serial killer rapist, said the *Los Angeles Times* again. These are all my trademarks when I was still in the Sparrow Unit in the Philippines."

"What's your point?"

"You know what? Up to now, nobody's known who was doing these things. And that's your gift—a master of disguise, who can vanish anywhere, anytime."

"Then?"

"Do you think Grace is alive and doing these things?"

"Why would you say that?"

"I told Grace a children's story about some people in remote places of the Philippines. They were a kind of people with mystical powers. Even when you decapitate and cut them into pieces, they would not die. The body parts would collect each other, attached themselves together, and presto, alive again. There were only two ways to kill them. First, you should take the head, run while the body parts were running after you, bumping into trees and bushes, stumbling along the way. You should be able to cross seven rivers. After the seventh river, the bodies will not be able to find you anymore; and even if they found each other, they would not be able to connect themselves anymore, and then eventually they would die."

Natasha continued. "The other way to kill these people was,

148

you should cut them into pieces and then cook them." She paused and said, "Remember that modern cannibalism article I cut out when we were in rehab? It connects everything."

"Why would you think it was Grace?"

Natasha showed him the front page of the *L.A. Times*. It was the picture of the man Detective Mark Fielder had seen.

"We must go to Los Angeles, California. All these things are happening in that part of the world. I have a gut feeling she's there."

"How do we find out and how do we find her, if ever?"

"You answer that. She vanishes the way you do."

"If she likes to disappear, no one could find her."

"That's because no one knows her, except for us. We're the only two people in the world she could not hide from."

"We were bedridden in the hospital for three months, a year in rehab. We asked everyone; no one ever found her or her body. Do you think she survived that blast in Oklahoma?"

"Who else has the guts to do those things and getting away with them? If it is not you or me, then who?"

"We'll find out. We go to America this week."

They booked a round-trip flight from Charles de Gaulle Airport to LAX.

LAX was swarming with arriving and departing passengers. The air was cool, an evening breeze coming from the Pacific.

They were escorted to their limo to the Hilton Hotel at Universal City.

At the hotel buffet, they started with fruit and salad then the main course, and last had the cookies and coffee as their dessert.

They had a long and warm shower together before they finally went to sleep.

In the morning in the lounge, Natasha and Anatoly were drinking their coffee. Natasha was smiling, getting the attention of

Anatoly and pointing to the big TV screen.

A man's face done by an artist was on the local channel's Breaking News. It was the face they saw on the front page of the *LA Times*, the face Detective Fielder has seen the night they survived the assassination attempt: the face of Resty. According to the newscaster, ". . . their ultra-modern, mixed martial arts, police expertise saved their lives and overpowered the killer."

It was a face well known to Natasha and Anatoly, the face of a clown, disguised as a normal person, but when peeled off, there's the face of a funny-looking clown, still hiding the real face of the performer, the childish face of their daughter, Grace.

Graconica Casilang Vasilevich: Missing since age fourteen, presumed dead. Now twenty-two years old. Known to her parents and friends as Grace. Known in the underworld as Resty. Known to herself as Nica, the lost girl.

The mother was presently known as Natasha Casilang Vasilevich, originally Maria Concepcion Silang, a descendant from the long line of the family of Diego and Gabriela Silang, the ferocious warriors during the Filipino revolution against the Spanish colonialists.

She studied as a full government scholar at the University of the Philippines. She joined student activists due to the growing dissatisfaction of the population against the corrupt government officials. She was recruited by and became the most accomplished assassin of the CPP-NPA in urban guerilla warfare, the Sparrow Unit, the elite group of the Alex Buncayao Brigade.

She left the organization when she found out that the CPP-NPA was more corrupt than the government she was fighting. She was disgusted that her effort and dreams died in vain.

She could not join mainstream society anymore. She had already committed many sins against her own people and against her own government, who cared about her and her future, which she had thrown away for nothing. She changed her identity, joined the circus, and traveled outside the country. Now, she must save her daughter.

The father, Anatoly Vasilevich, was born Mustafa Bisanovic. He was well known to his friends as Mustafa the Vanishing Magician.

According to the *Los Angeles Times*, Resty fell off or jumped out of the building, then vanished.

"Anatoly, this is one of your vanishing acts. If this Resty is not Grace, who could it be?" Natasha continued reading the newspaper.

"If that was not Grace, he would be sprawled, crushed to the ground. I only do that on a glass building where there is nowhere to hold so that it would appear that I vanished into thin air, and I have taught her well."

"How do we find her?"

"No. We don't find her. We'll show ourselves; then she'll decide on how to reach us without being seen. She might be in danger if we expose her."

"Let's talk to the manager of the Grove here in LA. We'll perform for free as a community service."

Anatoly called the manager's office.

"Thank you for calling the Grove, Los Angeles, California. My name is Karla, how can I help you?"

"Can I get an appointment to see the manager?"

"Sir, if you don't mind, whom I am talking to and what this is all about?"

"Tell him that a world-class magician and a world-class acrobat want to do community service by doing a million-dollar performance for free. And we want to do it at the Grove."

"Can you please hold?"

Anatoly waited patiently. After seven minutes of waiting,

151

Karla came back on the line.

"Hello, sir?"

"Yes."

"Sir, you may come to his office tomorrow at two in the afternoon. You come to the front desk, and we will take you to his office. Can I help you with anything else?"

"That would be all for now. Thank you very much."

"You're welcome. Have a good day."

He arrived the next day at two p.m. at the office of the manager, a young gentleman in a business suit.

Anatoly said, "This is a no-smoking area yet you have an ashtray."

The manager said, "You find it interesting. Show me something that will interest me, then we're in business."

Anatoly said, "You have a white and blue striped, folded handkerchief in your right front pocket. Can you please spread it on top of your table, take off your watch and fold the handkerchief to cover the watch."

The manager was intrigued. He listened, did as he was told, and said, "There it is. What's next?"

"Smash your watch with the ashtray."

"Are you sure you can pay for my watch?"

"Yes, sir. But not a brand-new one."

The manager did as he was told. He smashed his watch with the bottom of the ashtray.

Anatoly said, "Sir, put the broken watch inside your ashtray without spilling any piece out of the handkerchief, or your watch will never be returned to its original shape."

The manager carefully folded the handkerchief and put everything inside the ashtray.

"Now, sir. Your part is finished. It's my part now."

Anatoly, with one hand, put out a black handkerchief and

waved it to show that it was empty. Then he took the other corner with the other hand and covered the ashtray.

"Now, sir, open the bottom drawer of your table on your right, please."

To the manager's amazement, his Tag Heuer was on top of his neatly folded, white and blue striped handkerchief.

Anatoly took off his handkerchief from the ashtray and put it back in his pocket and said, "Check your ashtray, sir."

The manager did, and the ashtray was empty. He checked out his watch and handkerchief to his satisfaction, and said, "You're on the books. Live performance at the Grove."

The manager looked at Natasha. "What's the magic of the lady here?"

Natasha raised her right leg and placed it behind her head and did a backward somersault with one foot.

"You're equally amazing. Both of you are on. Friday night and Saturday night."

They left the room with smiles on their faces. Anatoly was touching the broken imitation Tag Heuer in his pocket, the one he had taken from the ashtray. It was the one the manager wore this morning because last night, the original was safely placed inside his office by a dark figure invisible to the guards and security cameras, invisible even to the security motion sensors.

Anatoly remembered the way he had escaped the Serbs in between tanks and ruined buildings. This one was a lot easier, without the live eyes and bullets. It was easier than escaping after he poisoned President Slobodan Milosevic in the Hague prison cell, a death befitting an infidel who slaughtered his own people because they had a different notion about God.

On Friday night at the Grove, the manager was looking at the teeming crowd of mostly mothers and children. He said to Karla, "I wish we had a bigger area for this kind of free entertainment."

The crowd enjoyed their performance, and word spread like wildfire.

Saturday night, everyone was elbowing each other just to get into the Grove. Three local TV news stations were on top of their platforms to cover the two-hour second day and last performance at the Grove of Anatoly and Natasha. Photographers from the *L.A. Times* were ready with their cameras and there were a lot of other cameras, big and small.

The LAPD and LA Sheriff Department assisted with security. The manager had to call them for assistance; their own security would not be able to handle a crowd as big as this one.

After their performance, Anatoly and Natasha went back to their hotel. They had a candlelit dinner.

Before going to bed, Natasha was picking the hair strands caught in her hairbrush. She rolled them in her fingers and knotted them into a special kind of shape. She went to the right corner of the room when facing the mirror, peeled off the corner carpet, and inserted the knotted hair.

Anatoly was watching and asked, "What's that for?"

"That's one clue that I taught Grace, if we want to trace each other. Surely there were some of those knotted hairs from her in every room she stayed, but we don't know where."

"Oh, that's why you were checking every corner of the carpet wherever we go."

"Yes, hoping that one day I would see knotted hair from her."

The next day, the couple was pictured all over the news, with interviews and appearances on local TV stations. Until their last day in America, Grace did not make contact with them.

They were leaving LAX for Charles de Gaulle at three twenty-five in the afternoon via Alitalia. They had a late breakfast at the hotel's lounge. The hotel transport was already outside and waiting for them.

Natasha asked, "Why did she not make contact?"

"We're not sure where she is."

"I'm sure she's in L.A."

"But you're not sure if she's out in the Caribbean for a sunny holiday, or India, or China. We'll never know."

"I'm hoping for the best." She stood up. "Let's go. I hate the airport rush."

They boarded the plane and suffered through the ten-hour and thirty-eight-minute, non-stop, long flight to Paris.

When they left Charles de Gaulle Airport, the black limousine they had called for was waiting for them. They were so sad and so quiet that they did not notice the tinted glass that divided the passenger from the driver. After two minutes of driving, Anatoly noticed something. Instead of going out toward his expected L'Autoroute du Nord they were going toward Goussainville.

But it was too late. Natasha was slumped and already sleeping, and he, too, felt the sleeping gas that he inhaled with the aftertaste of a mint. He felt his body went limp and before totally passing out, he heard they guy on the phone with the Serbian accent said, "Yes, we have them both."

The Discovery

Printed in the United States
142671LV00003B/7/P